THE JERUSALEM
FILE

Joel Stone

THE JERUSALEM FILE

Europa
editions

Europa Editions
116 East 16th Street
New York, N.Y. 10003
www.europaeditions.com
info@europaeditions.com

Library of Congress Cataloging in Publication Data is available
ISBN 978-1-933372-65-5

Stone, Joel
The Jerusalem File

Book design by Emanuele Ragnisco
www.mekkanografici.com

Cover photo © Steve Raymer/Corbis

Prepress by Plan.ed – Rome

Printed in the United States of America

CONTENTS

To my daughter
Katie
with admiration and love

THE JERUSALEM
FILE

1.

Let's begin this way. Levin went to the movies.

It was pure Hollywood, an action epic—the panoramic and the deeply personal—meaning widescreen violence and screw-tight sex, very good guys versus the world's worst, along with breathtaking special effects. Levin saw these dreadful movies once in a while, for reasons ranging from amusement to a malice toward pop America and her works. Today, he was primarily here to kill time.

But the movie couldn't quite kill enough. The sun was still shining when he came out of the moviehouse smack into Jerusalem's light. No place he knew had such a contrast between the darkness and the light . . . The sun glaring on old yellow stone. The shaded recesses of alleys and arcades. The uniform darkness of synagogue, church and mosque. God created light. But suppose not. Suppose light came first, and then the cool, consoling dark.

At a kiosk, he bought a copy of the *Holy Land Times* and took it into a cafe, going to an inside table well back from the sidewalk. The other patrons had the same idea. The rear tables were occupied, the front ones were not, a no-man's land in a sidewalk cafe. This was Jewish West Jerusalem, where people peered from behind coffee cups, on the watch for a man or a woman with extra bulk around the middle, or too-loose clothes, or fast nervous eyes, or eyes so vacant they looked dead. It was a Jewish national game, picking out the Arab suicide bomber, adding up all the signs and praying that you were wrong. Nobody was exempt, because disguises were part of the game: the bomb might be hiding in the Yeshiva student's briefcase, or strapped beneath the Hassidic's long coat, or under the benign Bedouin's robe. Any treachery was possible. So when a pregnant Palestinian woman entered the cafe, in her headscarf and floor-length abaya, all heads immediately turned, even those of the two Arab waiters. This was rare enough to be alarming in Jerusalem, a lone Arab woman in a Jewish cafe. Levin watched from behind his open newspaper. The woman took a table in the back, waited quietly, and ordered tea. That was reassuring. In the dash to paradise, the suicider rarely stopped and sat down. And yet, the tension lingered: what was the woman expecting, what was the abaya pregnant with?

Near him, a quartet of Israeli teenage girls—did their mothers know they were here?—were chatting and giggling over dishes of ice cream. What sweetness, what innocence, except for their tight T-shirts, skimpy shorts and bared bellies. At his advanced age, what was Levin to do? He really and truly resented them, little sirens with trims of baby fat. They couldn't know the impact they had on a man, they couldn't. Or could they? It was undeclared war between their bare bellies and the Arab woman's bulging yet modestly covered one, with its promise of an explosion, of one kind or another, for Jewish Israel.

And then Levin was suddenly on real alert. His reason for being here, one half of it, had walked in, a stocky, thirtyish man, rumpled and bookish in a round-shouldered way, and in fact carrying a book, an oversized art book, which could be a genuine aspect of him or else something to hide behind. Levin knew both to be true. He was Weiss, an assistant professor, an art historian. Passing Levin, he sat down at a table in the corner, where he immediately ducked behind his opened book. Levin heard the waiter repeat his order for an iced cappuccino.

The big art book had a woman's portrait on the cover; Botticelli, said the title. It had no secret meaning for Levin. Perhaps it meant something to the parties in the case.

He had his *Holy Land Times* up in front of him and peeked around it the way Weiss did with his art book, not the first time they had sat in this type of situation. They were both waiting for the same event, the same arrival, and before very long she walked in, Levin's other reason for being here, a striking, well dressed woman, dark-haired, well tanned, age forty-two, Deborah, his client's wife. She went to the table next to Weiss, without hesitation, with nothing to hide behind either. For an instant, the Botticelli moved, Levin saw Weiss's bright, happy eyes, and felt a bit like scum, sitting here and spying on them. The waiter came. She ordered an iced cappuccino also, and then sat sipping it through a straw. Levin strained for something between them, a word, a sign, hands reaching under the tables. All he saw, when Weiss's head bobbed up again, was that he too was sipping through a straw. Side by side, secretly intimate, their parted lips were draining their glasses.

They were lovers, according to her husband, Kaye, his manic client. It was clear to Kaye that Weiss, in the plaintiff's words, was regularly fucking Deborah. They might appear in innocent play, like sipping through straws, exchanging side-glances in a shop, sitting at opposite ends of a bench. But it was all filth, all foreplay, Kaye knew beyond all doubt. He wouldn't be fooled. Second opinions didn't interest him. Levin's job was to prove that Kaye was right.

They connected here, but if the plot held, the cafe was only their point of contact, not their final destination. The plan would vary; this time, Weiss was the first to leave. Without warning, he closed his book, stood up, and walked past the empty sidewalk tables and up the pleasant, tree-lined street. Levin sat still. He knew that he had only to follow Deborah to have them both; and five minutes later, that moment came. He was sorry to leave, not merely because he was so comfortable here. He felt he was wasting his time, hunting for proof of the lovers' guilt. Besides, he wished he could have looked at the teenage girls a little longer. It was pretty shameful, that here he was, a more than middle-aged man, undone by clingy T-shirts and taboo baby fat. Not that he would ever touch them. But how nice to be in their vicinity, to store up the memory, and not let Kaye's obsession with Deborah take him away. They were so young. What a shame—what a shame it was, in every burning sense of the word.

When he was outside the cafe, Levin looked back. All was the same: the vacant sidewalk tables, the people sitting in the back, the pregnant Arab woman, the Israeli teenage girls. Body parts, both luscious and horrific, blew through his imagination, equally beyond his control.

Yet all seemed peaceful. The cafe was not suddenly blown up. The customers inside lingered and drank their coffee. The girls laughed and licked their spoons. Levin returned to the trail of Deborah Kaye, who was following Weiss to their love nest.

Around them—it was part of the picture—the epic struggle went on, the blood bath, the terror and the counter-terror, the good guys against the bad guys, the endless fighting, with the suicide bombers claiming credit for the breathtaking special effects.

J ews and Arabs. As enemies, they were made for each other. First of all, each had a long memory. Levin knew you always started with that. Then, each was absolutely in the right and had no trouble expressing it, with impassioned lips, hands, this or that century's weaponry. Add the fact, double-edgy, that they were physically alike, if you peeked under their beards and their clothes, Semites both, smallish, dark, dark-eyed, with the same easy to draw big nose. Abraham and Ibrahim. In a bathhouse, given the dual circumcisions, it wouldn't be so simple to tell them apart. Of course, their clothes were a different story, the more so the more basic they were: The black-hatted, black-coated ultra-Orthodox, town dwellers to the core. The head-swathed and sandal wearing Arabs, looking like nomads wherever they dwelled.

Their battle might go on forever, if the past meant anything, the holy Jews and the holy Arabs, laying claim to the same holy land. This was a battle of the truest of Biblical proportions: the vastness of the stakes and the tinyness of the terrain. For Levin, the only way to continue living here was to anticipate the worst, try to go unnoticed, and be uncommonly careful. Go about your business. Read about the Arab terror and the Jewish bulldozers and assassinations, take sides, even change sides, if only for a day. Don't despair at the anger all around you, since hearts that harden can also soften, maybe. Trust yourself. Follow your own good nose, Jewish or Arab, and you might end up all right. Of course, it helped to be one of the non-practicing, the non-believing, someone who thought that blowing up both the Dome of the Rock and the Western Wall would be a good start toward peace. Kick out the holiness. Plant grass and trees there instead.

It also helped to be retired, finally detached, from his life in government in the security service. The heroic days were far behind him. He had been on secret missions, armed and disguised, but in the later years had manned a desk as a faceless intelligence analyst. He was in no sense a detective, whatever people thought, and even if he now found himself trailing an adulterous wife for a jealous husband. His sole unpaying client was something of a friend, who had begged Levin to do it; but the man inspired Levin's sympathy less and less. Kaye might have been in a bad situation. But he was also obsessive and vicious. It reminded Levin of a movie in which a fanatic cornered his prey, saw him jump to his death, and immediately leaped too, in order to continue the pursuit into hell. Kaye could be capable of that. He was thirstily and hungrily jealous, which meant he wouldn't stop until his suspicion proved mathematically true. He would hound Weiss and his wife until it was. And then what? Exposure? Divorce? Something bloody? Levin was growing uneasy. Playing detective, he had become a player for real. Whatever the outcome, he could be responsible.

He had been two weeks on the trail. It had tempted him as something interesting and rather charitable to do with his time. But he should have foreseen the embarrassment. From intelligence analyst he had gone to the gutters—gone from being a secret eye to a private eye, by any measure a big step down. It was shabby work. One day he would track Deborah to the various stops she made, and the next day he would follow Weiss. He would wait outside the place where they were finally headed, seeing nothing physical, only the moving hands of his watch, while his mind filled up with porno guesswork. He didn't take his licensed pistol along; except for Kaye no one seemed dangerous. Instead, he had a loaded camera, a tiny one, at the ready in his pocket. Kaye of course wanted pictures, meaning pictures that were conclusively obscene, graphic guilt being the object of it all. Levin tried to discourage him about the pictures and the degree of snooping they would require. He honestly couldn't visualize himself crashing in on the couple.

Was this to be his retirement hobby? He moved in such narrow passages these days that being invited into someone else's life, becoming a voyeur for a man he didn't even really like all that much, had a perverse attraction—a strange logic.

Part of him said, "Get out now." but for some reason he didn't completely understand, the other part said, "Stick around. This could get interesting." But despite his training, there were kinks in this friend and this friendly favor he hadn't anticipated. For now, he asked Kaye to be patient, to rely on circumstance, such as the lovers taking a hotel room, or clinched in a parked car, or lying together on the beach—or never doing any of these things, which might at least clear them of adultery. It could be they were Platonic soul-mates, sharing a love for Florentine art, one of Weiss's classroom specialties, something approaching that. Kaye only laughed at the idea. He wanted pictures of what he logically assumed and coolly expressed, that Weiss was sticking it into his wife. Weiss was a filthy pig—*Veiss*, as Kaye sneered, obviously playing on the English sound of it, besides nailing him with Vice. Kaye had no end of witty commentary and moral outrage. All right—one picture. One picture of the lovers. To be fair, Kaye was entitled to that.

Deborah was half a block ahead of him, the distance that Levin normally maintained. He felt secure enough. So far, she and Weiss had kept to neighborhoods in West Jerusalem, busy Jewish streets where they wouldn't stand out, and where Levin didn't stand out either. Like it or not, he was built for anonymity, medium all the way round, medium height, medium weight, medium gray. Unlike the secret-eye days, his disguise now was his unadorned self, his only prop the *Holy Land Times*, which he could sit and hide behind, or swat flies with, or roll up and swing as he walked, as he was doing now. He had actually met Weiss once, but that was at a public event and a few years ago and clearly had been forgotten. Deborah he had never met at all. A youthful type, she had a free, loose walk in her smart outfit and high heels. She was a woman you would notice, with her curly dark hair, her tanned, squared shoulders. He could picture her on the deck of a sailboat, or playing a good game of tennis. She wasn't stunning, but she dressed splendidly. Today she was wearing a sleeveless white cotton dress and carried a small white-sequined purse, in contrast to the coffee-table art book that Weiss sweatily lugged around. She no longer practiced law, but she taught a class at the law school, so she wasn't completely idle. She might be bored though. Levin figured she would have to be pretty desperate, too. He couldn't fathom what she saw in Weiss, beyond his fawning attention and his being ten years younger, which shouldn't have been enough for a woman like her. But maybe it was. One never knew.

As she walked, she window-shopped, the expected things, dresses, jewelry, shoes, a fancy chocolatier. Looking in, she would stand with her feet apart and her hand on her hip. It was very likely just a mannerism, but Levin would look sharply around for Weiss, as if she were slyly posing for her eager lover. Their liaisons were made of moments like that, touchless, tantalizing, like the two of them sitting with their cappuccinos and sucking on straws. When he called them lovers, Levin still had no proof. But being suspicious of people kept you alert. Back in the service, hot suspects were filed with known terrorists, just to be safe.

Few Arabs mingled here on Jewish Jerusalem's streets, though many worked in the restaurants and shops, often out of sight, in the kitchens and small back rooms. What made it more pathetic was that they were happy to get the work. If this enraged them, they couldn't show it, not there on the job. But their hearts must have leaped when one of their own hit back, pushed a button, exploded a bomb—Levin knew they must, even if most recognized the horror. Sometimes it wasn't human not to be inhuman. The same was true on his own, the Jewish side too. Kaye, Deborah, Weiss, they were probably in sympathy with the Arabs, and could understand their longing for a homeland. Levin knew this because he moved in the same enlightened Jewish circles. But when the Arab bomb struck, all that went up in smoke. The tribes of Israel could turn savage too, and bomb and bulldoze in revenge.

As she looked at shoes and chocolates, was she thinking about sex and Weiss? It was interesting how the flow, the story, was everything. If he merely passed her on the street, he would have given her a second glance, beyond a doubt. But would he be visualizing her about to strip off her clothes and totally abandon herself to sex? Probably not. As a cheating wife, she amassed sexuality, took it on as a sinking ship does water. Her walk in high heels dripped with it—her curly dark hair seemed dampish, a little like prying into her lower, tangy patch of mossy hair. Levin honestly didn't think he would use the camera. But he wouldn't mind having the opportunity to use it, being that close to the intimacies of Deborah Kaye.

She went into a jewelry store. Perhaps she wanted to escape the heat, or to browse and fill in time. She had been glancing at her watch, as if waiting for zero hour, whatever positive joy zero meant. Levin stationed himself at a bus stop across the street, pretending to read his *Holy Land Times*. Bus stops were notorious terrorist targets. If a bus came, or a queue formed, he would move; meanwhile, nobody coming or going had the look of a suicide bomber. By its name, the jewelry store was Armenian, so you could call it neutral ground, neither Jewish nor Arab, although how risk-free it was depended on the meaning of risk. An Armenian himself had warned Levin: "Never buy jewelry from an Armenian."

Jerusalem was full of warnings, not all of them so clear-cut. Two uniformed Israelis with slung rifles passed by, smoking cigarettes, probably guards at a nearby bus terminal taking a break. People had clashing feelings about their police and soldiers. On the plus side, they stood for order and protection. But for the same reason, they were the bullseye of choice for the suicider. If you could help it, you didn't want to get too close to a uniform. And they in turn were wary of who came close to them. Every day, everywhere, it was that sort of situation.

Kaye had told Levin: "Watch out. She smokes a cigarette after she makes love. It's virtually the only time she smokes. You may find that helpful."

Helpful—Kaye's peculiar approach. He was so eager to be helpful, to light Levin's way, to make success—catching his wife fornicating—as easy as possible. Kaye had other helpful hints for Levin. "She has no real limits. She's available anywhere. But she prefers the afternoon, around twilight, before it gets dark. She says it's more thrilling, less married, that way. At that point, anything goes. It's an automatic reaction—when she gets hot she goes out of control. I won't lay out the details. But you should be damned watchful at that hour."

It was getting to be that hour. The street was growing shadowy, cooling down. Some of the shops were closing. There would soon be a rash and cautious kind of night-life here. Deborah Kaye came out of the jewelry store. She stood in front of it, quite still, holding her sequined purse tight to her chest. It made Levin think that she had just purchased something precious. A couple of people were behind Levin, waiting for the bus, but he stood there, watchful, as still as she. It was twilight. She looked wound-up, tense. She was conceivably ready for an extra-marital thrill. If his operational intelligence was correct, something should happen now. They should be heading to their rendezvous.

Then he saw Weiss—coming around the corner of the street—walking in the direction of Deborah.

She had been in the jewelry store for twenty minutes. It was enough time to browse, enough time to buy, or enough time to do love, if that was how you came prepared to do it, fast and furiously on the sly. Would the Armenian have a back room? Of course he would. Every store had a back room. Many had a back door.

The magically appearing Weiss had stopped on the corner. Deborah Kaye now opened her purse, took out a cigarette case, tapped a cigarette and lit it. Then, Weiss had a cigarette in his lips too, and was igniting it with shaky fingers, cradling his big art book, sweating under his arms. They stood far apart, taking long, deep puffs, breathing out the smoke, their eyes darting at one another. She was sweating too, but in a dewy way. Ladylike.

It had already happened. Levin knew it. Quick as kids, they had made back seat love in a back room. Now they smoked—in their souls, smoked together. They added this almost languorous time as they drew out the thrill, smoking a cigarette for each other out on the street—at twilight—just as Kaye had said.

Perhaps there was a bit more tenderness to it than Levin had been led to expect. But tender or not, it had happened. That was his conclusion, although he couldn't prove it, not with the logical certainty that Kaye required. There might never be that kind of Einsteinian proof—never an end to this kind of job.

But when the two of them stepped on their cigarettes, in a simultaneous act, and slowly parted in opposite directions, as the sun finally set on Jerusalem, Levin tossed his *Holy Land Times* into a trash can and abandoned the bus stop. He considered that his day's work was over.

3

Kaye was Professor Jacob Kaye, but no one called him anything but Kaye. Levin found himself wondering, a little uncomfortably, what it was that moved people to drop their individual identity and be known only by their family name. Was it that they didn't like the person they were named after? They didn't like themselves? Whatever it was, he had to admit, it was something that he, Levin, and Kaye had in common.

Kaye was in his office as prearranged, seated behind his desk, surrounded by texts, journals, papers, the perfectly circular world of higher mathematics. He was a professor at the great university where Deborah taught law and Weiss was an art historian.

An intriguing question was: did Kaye ever leave his office and notice that he lived in a dry little sun-baked land? Far from sun-tanned, his face had a light, yellowish pallor. You could say he had a moon-tan, if there could be such a thing. It was a smooth face, that looked as if he never had to shave. He was smooth, clever, urbane, had never been young-looking and had not really aged for as long as Levin had known him. They were long-time acquaintances, but not real friends. In their present intimacy, as private-eye and client, it astonished Levin that he had once considered Kaye to be over-civilized.

"So they met twice," Kaye said with a self-satisfied smile. "That's beautiful. Twice is double the deceit, double the fun."

"Strictly speaking," said Levin, "they never met at all. They sat at separate tables in the cafe. Then they appeared a distance away from each other on the street. That's all I can tell you for certain."

"You're so right, my friend. We don't jump to conclusions. One step at a time. That's the way to nail them. I have to say I'm disappointed that you didn't get a single picture."

"Of what?"

"Something. The two of them sitting so close in the cafe. It could be the opening picture in the album. Why not?"

Levin let the absurdity speak for itself. He was occupying the chair where one of Kaye's students might sit, which could help to explain Kaye's air of arrogance. It was annoying, but Levin was inclined to be tolerant. It wasn't his wife who was cheating with another man, not Levin who was holding onto his shredded self-respect. As dark as the night was outside, Kaye's window shade was up. Levin took that as a sign of his consuming inner distraction. The quiet university campus wasn't as safe or simple as it seemed to be, because nothing in Jerusalem was. The university itself was divided. This was the mathematics and science part. The older campus, the setting for Weiss and Deborah, stood on a hilltop some distance away. There, a few months ago, a terrorist had left a bomb in a back-pack and blown up the cafeteria.

"While they were side by side," Kaye was musing aloud, "if you weren't watching, and he reached under the table, could he have passed her a note?"

"I never stopped watching."

"Yet they knew where to go next, where to complete their business. It's all been planned beforehand. They don't fuck on sight. They meet at point A first. Then one of them leaves and the other one follows. They meet again at point B. In the future, they might work in a point C. By the end of it, they're both in a frothing frenzy. Today, their last stop was the jeweler. There's no question about that."

"None."

"And she was in the jeweler's, what did you say, for about twenty minutes?"

"I'd say exactly twenty minutes."

"The blood-sucking Armenian, he must have rates. Did you inspect the place? Is there a back door? I'm trying to get the whole picture in my mind."

"Yes, there's a door—probably the back room—and an alley that leads around to the front."

"So after she comes out, Veiss exits via the rear and comes strolling merrily around the corner. He doesn't make any secret of it. He's just had his filthy hands all over her. But there they stand. Suppose one of our friends was passing?"

"They were very far apart. I doubt that anyone would have noticed."

"Did she ever smoke a cigarette?"

Ah—the question. Levin hadn't spoken of the cigarettes. He knew he should have, but Kaye seemed a man almost out of control. Levin had found himself protecting Deborah and Weiss, the guilty lovers, from the fiendishness of Kaye.

"Yes," Levin said finally, "she did, now that I recall."

"When was that?"

"Outside the jeweler's, after she came out."

"After! What did Veiss do?"

"He smoked too."

"Veiss? Veiss doesn't smoke. Did he choke?"

"I'm afraid not."

"The bitch, she's teaching him to smoke. It's like school. They take turns teaching different subjects. Now you see why we can't feel safe until we have at least one picture."

Kaye picked up his phone and dialed with a suddenness that could have no good outcome, whoever was being called. Levin looked the other way. But there was no actual conversation. After many rings, Kaye slammed down the phone.

"Of course she's home. She knew I'd call. Let's put it this way. It's either Veiss calling or me. She's torn—she's right by the phone. At the last second, she decides it's me. But she can't bear to hear my voice, not so soon after being with him. So she doesn't answer. She'd rather lie to me later that she was out of the house, out shopping, or at the law library, lies difficult to disprove. Of course, if she answered, I'd have hung up on her. Then she'd sit there and go mad wondering. Was that my Veiss baby? Why won't he talk to me?"

Kaye gazed off into space, into the future, into the past, who knew. Levin thought he spied tears forming in Kaye's so-sharp eyes, against his moonish pallor.

"Levin, I'd give my soul to be free of all this. All of these precious insights and deductions. Do you think I enjoy my brilliance? It's not the wonderful gift you would imagine. There are days when I yearn to be an ordinary man, going ignorantly about his business, like a dog without a nose, oblivious to the stink around him. Not to have to think and wonder. Just to live and let live. Not to have to know."

Levin jumped at his chance. If what he was hearing was true, he might not have to go on hounding the unsuspecting lovers.

"Should I stop following them?" he asked.

"I should say not. This isn't about me, my friend. We're talking about truth, and truth is never personal. It's implacable by design, like the evolution of the species. Truth—knowing—the burgeoning brain. It always leaves behind a cracked skull."

Levin had worked with mathematicians in the service. They were outside consultants for the most part, called in to decipher a code or solve some other type of problem. Supposedly, many mathematicians did their best work before they grew up, at some point between counting their toes and graduate school. Maybe it was true, and their new glimpse of reality had everything to do with being immature. But they were experts at puzzles, whatever their age. So perhaps the pieces fit and Kaye was right about point A and point B and all the intricacies connecting Weiss and his wife. The two were almost certainly having a love affair. The big unknown in the equation was Kaye—his pursuit of the affair, his relentlessness—the drift that made him so dangerous that Levin feared for Deborah and Weiss, a woman and a man he didn't even know. Why would a husband want proof that his wife was unfaithful and accept no proof that she wasn't? Was it the human need for certainty, multiplied in the case of a mathematician who was also a man obsessed? Levin knew how harrowing doubt could be. Always fearing. Never knowing. Doubt was dread. Doubt was the whisper that, in a dream, made you throw yourself off the cliff rather than stand and look down.

The suspense is killing me. Surely not. Surely suspense didn't kill. But it could make you ache to kill, either yourself or somebody else. Remove the doubt—take the leap. Living in Jerusalem made it all the worse. Everyone lived on the edge of the unknown. Board a bus, sit in a cafe, expect a bomb—strap on a bomb. That, the suspense in the suicide bomber, was unimaginable. Now? Now? Didn't he push the button, at last, in order to end the suspense?

His marriage had ended rather like that, abruptly, after their children were grown, when both of them discovered they had been wondering about ending it for years. It made for a happy divorce. They liked to say it enabled them to remain friends. But they weren't friends, they were old opposites whose paths sometimes crossed. Both were born here, but her sabra roots were deeper. Her parents had fought the British before they fought the Arabs. Levin was less committed, less political. Though he had made a career in the government, he looked back to Europe, to France, his father's homeland.

Through the years he dreamed about retiring there, France—Paris—the center of the world. Then he tried to persuade her. They were still at odds about it when they divorced, and that was well before his retirement, so the issue must have stood for much more.

But then, when he was finally free to go, Levin stayed. He was through working, his wife was an ex-wife, his children were usually abroad, his very aged parents were already provided for, in their separate ways. But by now, he had lost the will, the energy, to pick up and change his life. He felt too old. It was emotional and it was physical, and since he had no patience for the spiritual, that exhausted everything. Paris stayed a dream. The dreamer stayed in Jerusalem.

Even then, he might have accommodated himself, lived out his days passably, if Jerusalem had been one of the spent old cities of the world, a museum of a place, like Venice. By all appearances, it should have been, but frighteningly it was still alive. It had all the vital signs, the pulse, the breath, the veiny brain, and plenty of blood, more blood than water. It still bled—the world's oldest wound—and likely it would never scab over, not with so many fingers picking at it, so many, over so long a time.

4

T he lovers had so far kept to West Jerusalem for their not quite unobserved meetings. Today, Levin followed them into East Jerusalem, what guide books often called "the picturesque Arab half."

Among fellow Jews, they could lose themselves by appearing outwardly much the same. Here, they looked completely foreign. But on the other hand, no one was apt to recognize them in Arab Jerusalem and perhaps give them away. As Jewish lovers, they were in that sense safer here, reasoned Levin, unless someone reacted to them out of sheer resentment and hate. Picturesque, among other exotica, meant crowded, simmering, poor.

They met in the most public of places, an outdoor market-place. They weren't the only outsiders who had found their way here. Some Americans and Europeans picked through the bargains, from stall to stall. But the lovers weren't difficult to keep in view. Deborah Kaye wore a white and azure dress and a shady wide-brimmed hat. Weiss had turned up in a surprise white linen suit. More than tourists, they looked like British colonials from the past, out slumming in the bazaar. Weiss even carried a walking stick, not that cumbersome art book, but it didn't make him look any the more elegant. His white suit was rumpled and he used the stick oddly, with a kind of forward lunge. It gave a force to him that Levin hadn't seen before. He might be clumsy and fawning, but he could also be bluntly animal in a way that Kaye the husband was not. What did that say about Deborah Kaye? Something fascinating, even if Levin couldn't quite figure it out. Somehow it made her stronger, more her own woman, more challenging, than if her lover were just a grateful young man.

All the world was a bargain—that was the mystique of the bazaar. The stalls were cramped and many, the goods piled high, the vendors eager and meek, giving the illusion that they were selling off everything they owned or could scrape up, and at sinking prices. Only tourists were fooled, and probably not all of them. But with the bloody uprising, the intifada, there were fewer tourists day by day, so perhaps the eagerness and the meekness were getting close to being real. Levin felt sorry for the vendors, nearly all of them men, and not just because they were Arabs. As an old socialist, though not so fervent anymore, he pitied anyone whose life depended on the marketplace. He knew that somehow, somewhere, there must be a kindlier way. But his sympathy didn't move him to buy anything. He kept his eyes alert and his hands free—no *Holy Land Times* either—in picturesque Arab Jerusalem.

The men in the stalls seemed not to notice Deborah Kaye. Still, they must have known when she was approaching, the striking woman, likely a Jewess, wearing the wide-brimmed hat. She ran her fingers under fabrics like cotton sheeting and silken scarves. She slipped gaudy bracelets on her fine, tanned wrist. She squeezed melons and smelled them closely. She shopped with all of her senses, like women everywhere, but she might have been less a spectacle if not for the presence of Weiss.

Weiss was always a stall or two away, he and his plunging walking stick, stopping to look at the wares in front of him, but with his real attention, his real gaze, sidelong. He touched the things she touched, the fabrics, the jewelry, the fruit—he was brazen. It was obvious to anyone that although apart they were somehow together, the man following the pretty woman and the woman inviting him to.

Levin knew they were on their way to their lovenest and only pausing here, stretching the excitement out. To end up where today? If they stayed in East Jerusalem, the choice was narrow—a dark doorway, a blind alley, an obscure hotel. It was possible that Weiss had a contact here, an Arab workman or domestic, willing to rent out an evanescent space. Or the contact could be one of the vendors in the bazaar, waiting to slip away with the pair or slip them an address or a key. Of course, the vendors all looked suspicious, once you started eyeing them that way: the same cropped beard, the skullcap, the baggy pants, the dusty sandals. Once upon a time, he had dressed in their clothes to deal them a lethal blow. As an agent on a mission, he had helped assassinate one of them. At moments like this, with Arab men, he still felt squeamish looking at their clothes, as if donning their clothes had brought him inside their skins.

They didn't know he was among them, a sometime assassin of an Arab brother. He appeared so ordinary, so plain and elderly, his usual medium gray. Weiss, by contrast, fixed their attention. What was it about Weiss? Was it his white suit—his stalking gait and purpose? The walking stick alone expressed something ugly, something harsh and insulting. Unjustly or not, even if you didn't know him, you would dislike him on sight. You would mark him as a man to bring down. If you were an Arab, you would be happy to assume he was a Jew.

What was inevitable seemed suddenly to strike. The Arabs made Weiss a target. It wasn't lethal. He didn't come down. He winced; he felt his cheek. Then his hand flew to the back of his neck. Looking startled and confused, he almost danced, like a man assailed by bees.

Little stones, tiny pebbles, were being thrown at Weiss. They came from opposite directions, neatly timed, tactical. Levin quickly spotted the throwers. Two small boys, wearing skullcaps, baggy pants, sandals, minus only the beards, stepped from behind the stalls, flung their stones, and ducked for cover again.

Jerusalem had no end of stones, round, flat, smooth, sharp, from AD, from BC—no end. These days, bigger boys threw bigger stones in fury. These small ones threw pebbles just for fun.

The vendors were laughing. They knew what they were seeing, the game, the make-believe, a kiddie intifada. They laughed because it was funny. They also laughed because the Jew couldn't fight back, not against little boys doing no real harm. The helpless Jew was looking spineless and stupid, right in front of the woman he was chasing.

Weiss seemed frozen. Perhaps he had seen the small boys, perhaps not. If he looked around him, he saw Arab men. When he moved, it was to turn in a complete circle, with his stick upraised, immobilized by fear certainly, but equally by rage. Taken together, they gave his eyes a look of blindness. Then the eyes found something, not a man, a pile of dishes, a stall with dishes piled high. He lunged and cleared them off the table with his stick.

Deborah Kaye stood nearby. She was surely frightened. Though her face showed nothing, her hand held fast to the brim of her hat as if she were standing in a wind. Levin would have to act if she were swept into it. He was undecided about his obligation to Weiss.

The owner of the dishes was being held back by his fellow Arabs. He was squirming in their grip and screaming at Weiss. But he was the only one yelling for blood, so perhaps the others granted the Jew his stupid rage. The little boys were nowhere to be seen. Weiss, retreating with his stick raised, had the presence to throw some money at the Arabs.

Then Weiss and Deborah Kaye, walking together, made their way out of the bazaar. Levin followed, but he stopped himself at the edge. He let the two go on alone. He had no stomach for pursuing them to the finish today. Both were badly shaken. Let them find some pleasure in each other's arms.

5

L evin had created a simple life for himself. His creation was not yet done.

His tropical fish were dying, one by one. In death as in life, they had become a nuisance to him, though a minor nuisance, being, frankly, fish. He fed them, kept their tank clean, kept an eye on them, but knew the end. Three black mollys were left, two goldfish; so which was winning the race? He didn't intervene and toss them all out. That would be playing God, and he was much too tender-hearted. Doing the worst things possible, that no decent human being would do—that was typically called playing God.

The tank stood on a table in an uncluttered living room. It was a furnished apartment. An unfurnished place would have been cheaper. But he spared no expense to keep his life spare, leasing sheets and towels from a laundry, eating his meals out to avoid shopping, cooking, cleaning up, all that.

And when the time came when there were no fish left for company, he wouldn't need the empty tank for staring into either, while sitting by himself. He could stare into space just as well, and avoid the upkeep, the responsibility. It was the same with people. He saw less and less of old colleagues, old comrades, and didn't miss them. He knew this wasn't normal, but why not view it positively, as a series of gains, the way a hermit might cut notches in a tree to add up his feats of aloneness? There was nothing spiritual about it, although he lived in the Holy Land. He was godless, faithless, and proud of it—he called it the gift of doubt. Being unsociable had nothing to do with a greater power outside yourself. He believed that in their hearts, all ascetics, even St. Francis, knew that.

Miriam, his ex-wife, he still saw, but never on purpose. It was a jolt to discover they had chosen the same street to live on after their divorce. Here they were, together again. He found it extremely annoying, a reminder of the shared tastes that must have brought their stars into collision in the first place. She was often carrying a bag of groceries when they met. She had a regular apartment, stocked with their old furniture, and shopped and cooked in her usual way. If she wondered how he existed without her, she never inquired about it. They chatted, they weren't unfriendly. But if one spied the other from a distance, he or she might cross the street to avoid the looming exchange. They frequently talked about the children, their grown son and daughter. In contrast to him, she wrote them letters and saw much more of them, but that was natural, since she always had. Levin hadn't been a great father. His secret-eye work usually came first. Now that he had no work, and questioned the worth of that entire endeavor, he thought about the children with regret. In a way, it made him feel like a real father—his regret—for perhaps the very first time. Such regret also made him feel classically male, one of the few things that still did. So it wasn't all sorrow and pain.

He wasn't lonely, somewhat to his amazement. Of course, he didn't stay home all day and sit in his armchair and doze. He would have gone hungry if he had. There were restaurants to eat at, cafes for coffee, streets to walk along to get there. But that left a lot of new time to fill, like being promoted to heaven and starting an after-life. He didn't miss women, though there was that eye-twitching interest in pretty teenage girls. Shocking. But who didn't bathe in impulses they would never act upon? Listening to Kaye's urging, and shadowing Deborah Kaye and Weiss, that could have come from idle hours and boredom. It could have been an aging man's hankering for his old life, even when his life had been spent in the shadows. Either way, that little diversion was just about coming to an end.

He was withdrawing from his place and time, Levin realized, from the Jerusalem that went on around him; withdrawing in the only sane way he could, into the past. Scholars, collectors of things, many men had done it. Call it a time-tested idea. The past was always perfect, being done with, unchangeable, no matter how rudely cut off. The *Unfinished Symphony* was perfect, being unthinkable as anything else. The Venus de Milo had attained perfection, armless as she stood. So had the ravaged Parthenon, the noseless Sphinx, and every ancient ruin. The same with Jerusalem. How to live here—Jew, Arab, Christian, that was everybody's problem. It could be done, Jerusalem could be ideal, if it was the Jerusalem of the past.

Make a museum of it, like Venice. Why not? So much of it already was, thanks to all three Gods. His notion had somehow come to him, maybe a long time arriving, maybe only yesterday. He could be serious or playing a silly game. Make a museum of Jerusalem. Ancient history. That's what the tourists did.

He bought a guide book, the thickest and best. Everything was mapped out beautifully for him, the Old City, its twisting streets and glory gates, like the Damascus, the Jaffa; the separate, sacred precincts, belonging to David, Jesus and Mohammed; the oldest levels of the place, with their deep-dug sanctums and caves . . . The book's prose was purplish, yet not untrue. Some places he knew very well, some vaguely from boyhood, others not at all. But Levin had to be careful. The guide book didn't warn you which sites were still alive. If you went, say, to the Wailing Wall, you would see Jews pinning today's hopes and prayers to those poor, surviving stones. If you walked a short distance, to the domed El-Aqsa mosque, you would see Arabs in their own holy place, sending up their own prayers, often in mortal conflict with the entreaties on the nearby Wall. And on some days you might witness the sort of thing he was so sick and tired of—police clubbing away at a menacing crowd, soldiers arriving to defuse something, a bomb, or some gunswiveling hit man for God.

Take your guide book and start your tour, where else, with the museums. In Jerusalem the past was everywhere, but a museum walled it up for you, tied it down, so it wouldn't jump you by surprise. A museum was almost by definition dead, but in a good way, not at all depressing. It was also a way to escape the light, Jerusalem's fingering light, that always felt so personal. Guide book in hand, Levin began with the high walls, deep shade and restful benches of the Tower of David Museum.

He may have been in the tower years ago, before it was a museum, with his parents or on a school outing. He couldn't be sure. Most of it was an ancient ruin, reminiscent of other ruins, some of it battered and roofless—all walls and sky. In its day, it had been Jewish, Christian and Roman. King Herod built a ritual bath here. The Romans came and engineered it into an imperial pool. The Byzantines drained it and made themselves a quarry. An ancient ruin could restore your faith, if it wavered; that is, your faith that nothing was sacred, since your faith was your doubt.

The Tower of David Museum with its dioramas and treasure hunts hadn't yet realized that David had given them the slip. There was no sense of him left here, not the slightest, a disappointment to Levin. David was the only Biblical character he liked. How could you like Abraham or any patriarch? They were as stiff as boards, as hard as rock, all of them. Of course, they had never existed, nor had David, some scholars said. But he came out of someone's heart, a human being, real clay, and more than half pagan, like Michelangelo's naked colossus of him.

He might come back to David's place, where David was always out. Sitting on a bench, he felt very much at home. The gutted ruins were even less furnished than his apartment, and a lot more interesting, a good beginning. He felt encouraged. There were many other museums to visit, not just in Jerusalem, but Tel Aviv, Haifa, Jaffa and elsewhere. They could be Jewish, Christian or Muslim, for all he cared, and beyond the museums waited other promising excursions into the past. The Dead Sea, for example, could be a soothing experience, if it lived up to its name. Levin wasn't being sardonic, not entirely. He had found a way for a solitary, aging gray man to kill his time.

For just a moment now, he thought he saw Deborah Kaye here at David's museum. She was standing at the far end of the excavation, between the jagged walls. She was by herself, her back to Levin, that lithe youthful view of her that he had followed for days, and wearing her wide-brimmed hat. What was she doing here? What interest could she possibly have in the dead—this woman so full of life? He got up from the bench, not knowing why, but then the woman turned and it was a different woman. He had conjured up Deborah Kaye out of a hat. Was he disappointed? If he was, he also felt relieved, not wanting any of that messy business intruding on him here.

6

Another Jew had been shot while driving on a lonely desert road outside Jerusalem.

He had been on his way to Jaffa, to an out-of-the-way hotel. It was late at night, and a room had been reserved for him. His name was being withheld, pending notification of his next of kin. First reports indicated that he had stopped on the road or been ambushed, another victim of a random terrorist act. He had been shot with an assault rifle at close range. Police were seeking witnesses.

Levin saw this account of Weiss's death in the *Holy Land Times*. He read it with his morning coffee, never dreaming it was Weiss. But about the same time, the police were at the university, looking for the names of relatives. Word of their visit spread quickly across the campus, from Central Office to every department, reaching Kaye, who telephoned Levin.

"Veiss is dead."

"What?"

"The one in the paper, shot in his car. The police are here. It was Veiss. Driving to a hotel in Jaffa. I wonder why."

"Who did it?"

"The Arabs, presumably. One of those senseless acts. Though who are we to say what makes sense."

Levin wasn't feeling as steady as he had before. His sole wish was to hang up the phone. "I appreciate your calling. Thanks for letting me know."

"You realize you're off the case now. I mean, my wife. After this, there is no case."

"Clearly. I hope that everything works out."

"The swine was going to Jaffa to wait for her. I just this second got off the phone—she was still home. She hadn't seen the paper. She was shocked, my mint-cool wife. She must have dropped her car keys. Naturally she didn't say she was going to Jaffa. But she was more than ready, getting wet, waiting for his call to come join him. Neither of them had any classes scheduled. They could fuck out there all day . . . The filthy two-faced swine. He waved hello to me yesterday. I'd say that this time the Arabs got it right. At close range too. But I suppose we shouldn't speak ill of the dead. We should just let it sink in slowly that they're dead. Levin, my heartfelt thanks to you, for everything you did."

He was finally gone. He was so obscenely graphic about his wife, even when he couldn't possibly know. Why? Did it pain less if he stated facts, listed details, looked the demon in the eye? He was obsessed. But maybe there was salvation, relief, a comfort side to obsession. You could feel in control of the worst . . . Levin imagined Deborah Kaye suddenly getting the news. Then he thought about Weiss in his car. That suddenness.

He fed his few fish. He didn't exactly connect Weiss with keeping one more fish alive for one more day. But fellow-feeling for another human was hard to contain, even if you didn't much like the fellow concerned. Just let it be someone you knew and it automatically spilled over you. It wasn't compassion. Levin couldn't say what the hell it was, but fear wasn't far from it. He would be surprised if Kaye wasn't feeling unsteady too, along with his gloating hate.

He needed some fresh air, which was pretty funny, since fresh air, open space, was what he instinctively feared most. But he went out, walked through the neighborhood, stopping in a little green park with a playground, where mothers took their children. Levin might have been the only one there who was surprised that such places still existed in this city. He sat down by himself on a bench. He was in Jewish territory, not far from home. That helped. So did the sight of the big policeman, keeping an eye on things. So did the mothers and children—the mothers because they protected, the children because they were being protected, as if a place with mothers and children must be a totally safe place. He felt very old. He wasn't afraid of dying. But would he be sitting here like this—surrounded by women and children—if he weren't a certified old man?

He wasn't really so ancient, only nearing sixty. But unlike men who exercised, ate wisely and wore youthful clothes, he looked his age, rather drab and gray, but a gray man, he liked to think, with a rainbow mind. People were amazed to hear that both of his parents were here in Israel, still alive, though in his father's case it was only a formality. Anna and Joseph . . . They belonged to the near-mythical generation, in its unforeseen way the very first, the boatloads of Jews brought out of holocaust Europe. You could still see them close-up, in the synagogues, in nursing homes. In their hearts, in their bones, they were still refugees, the children of Europe, more than of Israel. That was their Jewish identity, whatever their papers said. Though here for sixty years, they had never ceased being refugees, tossed from the sea, still lashed or clinging to their old European world. . .

Anna lived on the outskirts of Jerusalem. She lived alone, behind tall locked gates and a double-locked door. She had a tiny apartment. Levin could still be startled, finding such a lively little character in such a small confined space, her two rooms crammed with things from the larger past; framed family photographs covering every wall; crocheted white doilies wherever a doily could be thrown. There had not been room for the piano, but the bench was there, with a doily, on which sat a samovar, bought in East Jerusalem at an Arab bazaar, to bring back memories of Russia, bitter as the memories were.

She's like a little canary in a cage, Levin thought . . . a canary with a mate who was in another cage, not far away, that cage being a hospital ward for the demented. Separately, they lived out the ends of their lives, two very small people, who had been unwillingly awesome when they graced the same room. Joseph had been shipped by the Nazis from France to Auschwitz. Across the map, Anna had survived the Nazi siege at Leningrad. Thanks to all that, they had met and married here in the Promised Land.

Levin brought her a jar of salted almonds, her favorite snack. She opened it, sniffed and sampled a few, and stored it away in the cupboard. As usual, she brewed tea for them, real tea from leaves, but not in the samovar, too big a bother for two. She served it with wafer-thin slices of lemon and dripped raspberry jam into hers. Her radio was playing in the background. Levin could be sure she knew about the latest terrorist killing. She seldom went out, and she didn't read the newspaper. But she had her radio. Her radio was her closest friend and her closest enemy, on all day long.

"Why is this different from Leningrad?" she wanted to know. It was her favorite question, often asked, and as usual she tried to answer it. "All right. In Leningrad we starved, that's true. We were hungry and thirsty and filthy besides—while they were at it, they bombed the bathtubs and toilets too. They were the Nazis. What would you expect? They were monsters, roaches. But we kept them out. They never got inside. Not one. It was a siege. There was a line.

"There was a line. Not like here. Here, a Jewish man gets into his car, gets Jewish gas, drives on a Jewish road, from one Jewish town to another, and they wait for him and shoot him. What's the good of a Jewish homeland? To be together? They were together in Auschwitz. What was the good of coming here? Why is this different from Leningrad?

"I'm not so sorry for myself. I'm an old woman. I've had my slice of life, though I never thought I'd be back where I started, practically, afraid to walk to the corner and take the bus. How can anyone be a suicide bomber? What kind of upbringing did they have? I hear their mothers are proud of them, but I don't believe it. That would make the mothers even worse, to be proud of children like that. And then, to think about your child blown to bits, those fingers and toes, that you brought into the world. I have nothing to say to those mothers. I hate them. They should expect to be hated. Who are they, these people? Where did they come from, out of the ground? Haven't the Jews suffered enough? They didn't need the Arabs to prove it. We weren't all saints but we were good people. Better than good. That's why we were allowed to come here. We were supposed to be left alone and live in peace. Now I'm afraid to go to the store. Why is this different from Leningrad?"

She stared into her teacup and stirred up the jam. Quiet like that, she might have been thinking about Joseph too, the other bad ending of her life. She picked up her cup with both hands and drank. She was a strong woman. Levin could feel her strength even now, as tiny and old and besieged as she was. It was hard for him to come away.

He never mentioned knowing Weiss, the Jewish man shot in his car. Her own little radio would bring enough terror home.

7

L evin skipped the funeral. As it turned out, Weiss had no family here, only relatives in America, where it seems he planned to emigrate some day. But plenty of people came to say good-bye. As a terrorist killing, it was a national event. Besides Weiss's colleagues and friends, the political and religious troops were there, strangers to the martyred Jew, but eager to lend him their grief and outrage.

Levin was familiar with such funerals in Jerusalem. The Arab side had them too, when the Jews could be called the murderers. If anything, the aggrieved Arabs were noisier and angrier, with men hoisting and marching with the casket and the crowd beating their breasts. It must be the Western influence, Levin decided, that kept the Jewish funerals more quiet, more quiet and refined. Was that progress? Perhaps. The Arab send-off seemed raw Old Testament, tribe-driven, as if Ibrahim still went into the ground the way Abraham once did.

He dodged Miriam too. He saw her coming and ducked into a bakery, staying there until she passed by. The bakery smelled good. Fresh-baked bread. His best experience of the week. He bought a loaf and ate a chunk walking down the street, which he hadn't done since he was a kid.

He found himself comparing Miriam with Anna, his ex-wife and his aged mother. It was no contest. For Miriam to stand a chance, Anna would have to be his ex-mother. There were other obstacles. Miriam had her virtues but she was stubborn, opinionated, and mired in her Jewishness. Anna had her flaws but she was strong-willed, outspoken, and had a quaint old worldliness. There was an odd symmetry about it— Miriam's flaws and Anna's virtues—Levin noticed that. Yet they were completely different women, pumpernickel and rye, two completely different recipes. Sometimes he wondered whom Miriam compared him with. Her father? She might do that. He was long dead. Or was she seeing another man, Miriam—his amputation—at her age?

It was a long day, still the day of Weiss's funeral. As part of the university crowd, Kaye and Deborah Kaye would no doubt be in attendance. It would be interesting to see them together, grieving over Weiss. There was still time for Levin to go.

He decided otherwise. He had a better idea. He had an Arab friend, or at least acquaintance—Ali—a Jerusalem Arab, but no zealot, smart, open-minded, a counterpart. Take wretched Gaza. Levin could joke that the only difference between hell and Gaza was that at least hell was paved with something, and Ali could see both the joke and the sympathy. They had that kind of easy relationship. On this day of Weiss's funeral, a day of general hate and personal weariness, Levin decided it was a good time to visit Ali and his family.

They lived in East Jerusalem, not far over the line, that line that was imaginary but far from being imagined. It was a different world, as the guide books said. Desert robes and kaffiyehs walked the streets, and veils and abayas. Old men sat in cafes, smoking their bigger than life water pipes. It was a poignant world, when the smell around the bend could be uncollected garbage or sweetly aromatic lamb. People squatted on the ground, in that way that told you the West had ended and something else began. You heard the amplified calls to prayer, bleating from on high, alien to Levin, eerie, and uncomfortably profound.

Ali had an ornate past: junk dealer, car mechanic, cab driver, tour guide and other pursuits as well. A man with a family, he went where the work was, but he was also a dreamer, so the vagaries of his life were hard to pin down. Levin had met him when he worked as a translator for the service. These days, he managed a cafe, with outdoor tables, an indoor restaurant, and his family quarters in the back.

They embraced on meeting. It was nothing unusual, but Ali was the first person he had embraced in a long time. Ali would have fed him if he hadn't already eaten. He fed Levin anyway, with fresh dates and a fragrant glass of tea. He had two young Arab waiters working, so he took time off and sat with Levin in a family room in back. "I know they look like terrorists," he said about the waiters. "But that's good. If I have Jewish customers, the real terrorists will think we're already on the bomb list and go away."

Levin laughed. They sat in a simple room laid with carpets, where he occupied the only comfortable chair. "How's the family?"

"Wonderful. Growing like weeds. And you? Do you have a lady friend yet?"

"That's why I came over here today. I'm looking for a nice Arab woman."

Banter—good friends' small talk. In the inevitable way, they moved to the political situation, the turmoil, the newest incident. Levin mentioned that he had known Weiss. He talked about Weiss's funeral, described it as if he had been there. He condemned the political passions. He ridiculed the orthodox crazies, denounced the greedy Jewish settlers and the shameless hypocrisy of the Jews.

Ali chimed in with the Arabs' responsibility, their stupid blindness, their leadership's corruption, the total insanity of their suicide bombers.

Levin could see what was going on. But he couldn't stop it—merely see it. The worse things got between their people, the better friends they felt they had to be, the more toleration and sympathy they had to show, and the more collective guiltiness, too. As friends, they were as stuck as enemies. Their friendship wasn't theirs anymore. It belonged to the struggle between the Arabs and the Jews. It wasn't friendship between two men.

Levin felt very bad. He would have felt worse if he thought that Ali also sensed what was going on. But he probably didn't. Nothing about Ali suggested that he was so sensitive a man, considering his menial past, his background. Levin was ashamed of himself for having this imperious thought, which made their friendship even more improbable. But he couldn't be confident of anything by now. What was the man sitting opposite him really thinking?

Ali's older daughter came into the room. Levin tried not to stare when he saw her. They had never exchanged a word, not even a hello. Why would they? She was an Arab schoolgirl, about seventeen now, shy, or seemingly. She wore a long loose dress. Her white headscarf made her face round, immaculate— a blank. Could a face and a mind really be as blank and innocent as that? She busied herself putting some things into a drawer. To her father she wasn't even there. She sometimes appeared when Levin visited. He flattered himself that she was curious about him, a Jew, a former Israeli official, once her father's boss. He was certainly curious about her, though it was hard to try to look at something when you were trying not to. He didn't believe she was the reason he was here. He didn't believe it. She was thrice forbidden to him—a schoolgirl, an Arab, his friend's daughter. Forbidden—easy to say. He could control his actions, but not what came into his head. Those old hermits who flagellated themselves must have known they deserved a whipping. If they were like him, what they were thinking was worth a whipping. In his discreet way, he watched her. Was she secretly watching back? And his Arab pal Ali—all three of them here—what was any of them actually thinking?

Levin sat a while longer. He kept hoping his awkwardness, his unease, would go away, and honestly, no one gave any hint of anything wrong. But he finally left, unsatisfied. Between the father—and the daughter—he probably couldn't come here anymore.

8

Levin had no car. He couldn't imagine his aging butt on a motorcycle, and he had taken his last blithe bike ride back in his student days. In Jerusalem, if he couldn't get there on foot, he took a taxi. He avoided all buses. A city bus, that former mastodon of civil order, was something to be feared, a rolling bull's-eye for the suiciders, especially if you were sharing a ride with your protectors, Israeli soldiers.

To get out of town, he would rent a car, filled with peril too, as Weiss's murder had freshly shown. But you had to travel in something, didn't you, and a car was under his own control, with the doors and windows close around him, and only himself as the moving target inside.

He was driving to the Dead Sea today. It had caught his attention when he was looking through his guide book. He hadn't been there in years, not since his parents took him to float on the magical salt water. True, it wasn't a museum, but never mind that. For his purposes, it was historically dead enough. You had to drive through miles of desert to get there. What you found at the end wasn't teeming with life either. It was a lake, geologically speaking. But no greenery surrounded it. Nothing lived in it. Scientists actually worried that it was getting deader, meaning that even the mud was drying up. The mud was the main attraction these days. People could still frolic on top of the salt water, but it was the mud that drew the visitors. Dead Sea mud was said to be good for the skin and soothing to the nerves. Medical specialists affirmed it.

Who wouldn't drive through a desert wasteland for wonders like that?

It was early, but people were already on the scene when Levin arrived, a sprawling tourist crowd, more humanity than he expected. Worse, they were a family crowd, which meant children. It was axiomatic to Levin that families and children spoiled an experience, domesticating it somehow, and in direct relation to their size. The Dead Sea, he saw now, was safe—too safe. People could bring their children. There weren't even armed soldiers when he gazed around, not a solitary one, unless they were patrolling in the desert out of sight.

He made the best of it, choosing a remote spot on the sand, far back from the water's edge. He had his shoes off and his trousers rolled up and had come equipped with a sun hat and sunglasses. But it was and it wasn't the same Dead Sea of old. Along the shore, where he remembered mud and sand, were beach chairs and beach umbrellas, their bright colors splashing. The Dead Sea, the lowest point on earth, a dismal lake that killed all life, had become a popular resort. At its edge, you could buy ice cream cones. In the background, not too far away, were cafes and hotels, plus boutiques selling jars and tubes of the soothing and beautifying mud. Freshwater springs waited nearby, for ceremonially washing up. So grown men and women, down below in their bathing suits, rolled in it and smeared their faces with it, the rejuvenating Dead Sea mud.

They had taken the deadness out of it—simple as that. The bleakness, the barrenness, the beauty, the quiet, were gone. He knew it was cranky to complain. Why shouldn't people and their urchins have their fun? But he complained anyway, as if he had set his heart on having the Dead Sea to himself, feeling what he was supposed to feel here. Call it a sentiment sacred to the unbeliever, a human connection to the ages. . .call it an old man's oneness with things as they always were and would be. Instead, he felt out of place, out of his time. They had removed the deadness from the Dead Sea. It wasn't a small thing. It seemed to him that he sat facing the question at the core of everything in this anointed land: Maybe the desert wasn't meant to bloom?

Now Levin saw that he hadn't retreated far enough. Even back here, he wasn't going to be alone. A woman had come out of the crowd at the water's edge and was walking in this direction. She wore a dress; but her face was covered with mud. She walked slowly and unsteadily in the pebbly sand, carrying her high-heeled shoes. Staring behind his dark glasses, Levin watched her coming nearer. She might have been young and attractive, she might have been something else. With the mud on her face, it was impossible to tell, though he guessed that like most women she was here for the sake of her skin more than her nerves. The tarry black mud made a mask of her face even as she drew close. Then her figure, her shoulders, her white neck—Levin realized that he had watched this woman before. It was Deborah Kaye.

What a coincidence, thought Levin, driving out to the Dead Sea and running into Deborah Kaye. She would never recognize him. He had always been careful following her, and today he was wearing a hat and dark glasses. But he was wrong. She walked right up to him and stood over him.

"You don't know me. But I know you," she told Levin.

He raised his hat brim and looked surprised. "Really? You know me?"

"Your name is Levin. You used to work in the security service. You know people I know."

People. That would surely be Kaye, Levin presumed. But he asked the question anyway: "What people do we know?"

No answer from the mud mask. Though shaky on sand, she was a self-possessed woman, Deborah Kaye. She had already sat herself down beside him.

She hadn't recognized him—Kaye had mentioned him,

talked about him. Why? Was it to savor the taste of naming the man who was secretly following her and her lover? That was perverse enough to be true, with Kaye. But she obviously had no idea of their collusion, the private-eye arrangement between Kaye and himself. She seemed to trust him, the security service man she'd heard about. More than that, she had tracked him down. She had some need for him. Why?

"You followed me out here today, didn't you?"

"That's true. Yes I did."

"I didn't see a car behind me. Believe me, I was watching. One always does these days."

He thought the mud mask winced. Weiss—lover Weiss shot driving on a lonely desert road. "I drove on ahead of you most of the way," she said. "After a while, I could guess where you were going. There's nothing else out here. If I missed you today, I'd try another way." She looked at the Dead Sea. "Do you come here often?"

Levin smiled at her. "As often as I can."

Deborah Kaye wasn't listening. Behind the mask, she was starting her story. "I have to talk to you. I need your help. It's about a man named Karl Weiss. He was murdered in his car. You must have heard about it."

"Terrible thing. Yes, I saw it in the paper. He was killed near Jaffa somewhere. Shot by terrorists."

"That's always what they say . . . the mindless terrorist act."

"Am I mistaken? Is there something about it that I missed?"

"Were you a spy for the government? Doing very secret work? To be frank, dirty work is what I heard . . . from the people we know."

Why disillusion her, a grieving woman? To be frank, he didn't mind Kaye portraying him so arrestingly. Besides, there was some truth in what she said, a small grain, a very long time ago.

"I can't comment on my service. I'm sure you can understand. I did spend some years doing intelligence work. I can tell you that."

"I don't think Karl Weiss was killed by a terrorist," said Deborah Kaye. "I can't give you any proof. I just don't believe it."

"If that's what you think, why don't you go to the police?"

"I can't do that. Don't ask me why."

"Was Weiss your friend?"

"More than a friend. He was my cousin."

Lie number one, thought Levin. Not that her lying offended him. It intrigued him, like her mud mask, another form of lie. She gave the impression that you could skip the mask and look into her eyes. Not so. Perhaps he knew too much about her. She was an unfaithful wife, she'd had at least one lover. At the same time, he knew nothing about her. So her lying fascinated him. Her deceit trailed like a perfume, a scent leading him on.

"What you want from me is to poke into this for you, apply my skills. In secret, of course."

"I can pay a lot. I owe it to my cousin. Please, I'm not a crank. I can give you some good places to start."

"Such as?"

"He was threatened—an Arab went after him in East Jerusalem at a bazaar. I was there. The university, that's another place. Karl was brilliant. He taught art, but there could be someone from another department, someone who had a grudge against him."

"Will you tell me who you are?"

"Certainly." She turned her cheek. "This silly mud, I know. It must seem ridiculous to you. But it's not you I'm afraid of. You'll see me all you want. My name is Deborah . . . I'm Deborah Weiss."

9

Another lie, another slap of mud on the Dead Sea face. The mud was primordial, a contrast to her modish dress—as she sat here beside him or, as before, advanced toward him holding her high-heeled shoes. It was a contrast but a match also, with her dark eyes, her full but flattened lips, her nearly pure Semite features. She could have existed in the Old Testament. She would have been one of the women dancing with a tambourine around the molten golden calf. The mud made her eyes glitter. Like any mask, it helped her to lie better. For her own reasons, she had sought him out: "I need your help. You'll see me all you want." Of course he said yes.

He declined to take any payment, because, he told her, he could make no promises. Also, because he wanted to "see justice done." Levin may almost have meant it.

They parted, with Deborah Kaye leaving him behind, just as she would have left Weiss, walking in the sand, on her way to the freshwater springs to wash her muddy face.

Kaye must be the one she was afraid of. He was the reason she couldn't go to the police, show such warm interest in Weiss. He was the reason she suggested the university as a place to find someone with a motive. The angry Arab wasn't a serious suspect. By insinuation, she was pointing to Kaye. And Kaye did possess the icy passion that, if it couldn't make him able to do it, made him capable of having it done.

What in hell had kept them together? Dull habit, like himself and Miriam? Levin pictured them, the roving wife and the obsessed husband, and didn't think habit was the answer. It couldn't have been the children, because there were none. Of course, Kaye was mad about her. But what did she get out of it? Kaye was very well-off, with family money. He was highly regarded in his field, if for his early work. In that ageless, academic way, he was a handsome man, though clearly older than she. Maybe his personality, the coldness, drew her, along with his jealousy, the heat. You could never be sure of anything with a husband and wife. Perhaps they weren't really together, and sleeping apart, or were in their final days together, and she was on the brink of leaving him. She mortally feared him, so for now she stuck with him. But she believed that he had murdered her lover, and she was trying desperately to have him caught.

When he told her, yes, I'll help you, what mirage could have been in Levin's mind? Back from the Dead Sea, out of her sight, he honestly didn't know. He had acted on impulse, an invigorating thing. But he didn't expect to find out who killed Weiss, whether it was Kaye or anyone else. He might be able to eliminate some possibilities, including Kaye, all but the unknown terrorist who had surely done it. He pictured the lethal Arab, by the side of the road, waiting there for any Jew. It wouldn't have surprised him, or made him lust for revenge. In these times, he couldn't completely blame the terror on the terrorists, though he kept this to himself. To be sure, the suiciders took getting used to, and it was a big shock when the women moved into it, blowing their bodies up. But he mostly got used to that too. He might miraculously track down Weiss's killer. But it wouldn't be for the sake of justice, or with any degree of hope, or any kind of plan. His search was probably a fraud. But call it a friendly fraud. Who suffered? Where was the victim? Deborah Kaye would be getting his loyal services, or otherwise none at all.

He decided not to try Security, his old outfit, where he was universally known. This was personal work, not to be entrusted to the professional curiosity seekers. Instead, he went to the Jerusalem police, where he knew them well enough to get access without engaging their interest. He was taken to the office of a veteran detective, an acquaintance, who sent for the Weiss dossier. Levin was fully prepared to be less than honest and he immediately got the chance.

"Weiss was a good friend of mine. We shared common interests. We went to art shows, museums, had lunch now and then, that sort of thing."

"There's not much I have here. He was driving to Jaffa, stopped the car for some reason, and was shot sitting in the driver's seat."

"At close range, the paper said."

"Very. With an assault rifle. It blew his head off."

"And no witnesses?"

"None we could find. Another car eventually came by, a Jewish family. They found him. They don't know anything."

"Nothing left at the scene, no evidence of any kind?"

"Just him. Just Weiss."

"Why was he going to Jaffa?"

"He had a hotel reservation. And no, we don't know why."

"You think it was a terrorist?"

"What would you think? He had no family, no women, no enemies, only friends. After they're dead they only have friends. Like you. You're taking a very big interest in this Weiss guy. Why?"

"No particular reason."

"No reason?"

"I knew him. That's all."

"How's retirement?" smiled the detective acquaintance, leaning back in his chair.

"Just fine."

"It must be great, having nothing to do all day, just poking around the town. It must really be great. Those museums, you do a lot of that? Great places, they tell me. And how about the movies? That's another great way to spend the afternoon. They're always changing them too. I've got a few years of this shit left myself. What a nice thing to have. Leisure time. But confidentially, I'm more the outdoor type. If it was me, on a day like this, I'd be out lying in the sun. Boy, wouldn't it be great . . . having nothing to do."

The detective smiled broadly, leaning back, hands clasped behind his head, looking smug, pugnacious. Maybe he was envious of Levin. Maybe the timing was bad and he was up to his balls in work. Maybe he was inherently nasty and Levin had never known it. But Levin felt stung. He hadn't come here to be greeted as a pest, an old geezer intruding on the serious business of life. The swipe about the museums and the movies, that punch really hurt.

Levin got up to go, keeping it all to himself. The irrepress- ible detective called after him: "Don't bother going to Jaffa. They won't know anything there either."

Everything was personal. That was the lesson. You could have the purest mission in the world. But sooner or later, one way or another, everything turned personal. The detective stung him with the recognition of the used-up man he was. Deborah Kaye imagined that the terrorist was her husband. His friend Ali showed him how they had no friendship. His mother kept a World War going in her kitchen. Growing old he had become more sympathetic toward the Arabs—weaker as a man, more in harmony with the weak and stateless Arabs. Everything was personal.

He took a taxi to East Jerusalem, an Arab taxi, considered safer there. He rode it to the bazaar where the Arab had tan- gled with Weiss. He was sorry he had to return. It wasn't only the sight of the people. It had something to do with the donkeys. The farmers hitched them to wagons or rode their backs into town to the marketplace. A man on a donkey was disheartening. The long-legged human astride the small animal made the animal pathetic. The overwhelmed little donkey made his rider seem pathetic. There were usually some lambs around too. Jesus may have been a Jew, and the Christ, but it was the Arabs and their animals who brought back the scene around the manger.

Unlike his first visit here, when he was following the lovers, today Levin wore a Muslim skullcap, baggy dark pants, a pair of sandals. If he spoke, his Arabic was excellent, with an almost indefinable accent. He had always been able to pass as an Arab. He didn't hurry. He browsed his way through one row of stalls then another, until he came in sight of Weiss's Arab and his tableful of piled dishes.

As he came nearer, Levin's eye went to a large serving plate in the center, a plate propped up on its edge. A picture was taped to it, a newspaper photograph, a photograph of a man, Weiss's obituary photograph.

Levin walked up to the stall. The vendor's hands flew about as he ritually pitched his wares. Levin picked up a dish. In Arabic, they talked price. The vendor said suddenly:

"You're a Jew. Why are you wearing our clothes? You think you'll get my dishes cheaper?"

"You're a clever man. Yes, I'm a Jew. But I often wear these clothes. I like them. I like Arabs."

"As I like Jews."

Levin pointed to Weiss's picture. "He was a Jew."

"He was. I liked him too."

"He's dead now."

"He is. Allah took care of him. I have his picture here to remember him."

"You knew him?"

"Allah knew him, as he knows everyone. So Allah took care of him."

The man laughed loudly. He spoke loudly, so that the other vendors could enjoy the joke too, the same joke all over again: Weiss's head on a plate. The head of the Jew who had smashed the Arab's dishes. The head that had been blown off by a rifle.

"You knew him, didn't you. He had some business with you," said Levin. "Something happened here."

The Arab stopped laughing, abruptly very cautious. "You're mistaken. We never met. I only do this in his memory. Do you want to buy the plate, Jew? Special price for you. Very cheap! But I will keep his head."

10

L evin looked at his investigation so far.

The Jerusalem police: There were no witnesses. There was no evidence. There were no suspects beyond an unknown terrorist. The only new and extraneous piece of information was that Weiss's head had been separated from his body, blasted off, or else the bullet spray had cut it like a scythe. Could be a ritual beheading. Could be just a bloody mess.

The Arab vendor: two versions . . . His dishes smashed, the enraged Arab hunts down Weiss, follows him to Jaffa, and kills him. Version two . . . The enraged Arab reads about Weiss's death in the paper, cuts the recognized picture out and gleefully exhibits it. Picture of head and actual loss of head a coincidence . . . Levin favored this version of events. Tracking Weiss down in a city this size would have been all but impossible. The offense, the smashing of some dishes, seemed a paltry motive for murder, though many had died for less. But Levin didn't see the vendor as a cold-blooded killer, just a very happy Arab whose wildest fancy had come true.

What next? What other unlikely avenue to pursue before he saw Deborah Kaye again? She had a plan for seeing him, as she had a plan for everything. Levin was to put a classified ad in the *Holy Land Times* saying that he had a talking gray parrot for sale. Then she would phone him and they would arrange a meeting. A talking gray parrot was unlikely to attract many calls, she said. But Levin also sensed something teasing about it, that he was her talking gray parrot. To tell the truth, it tickled him, being teased by a pretty woman who was young enough to be, well, his daughter. She had an unexpected sense of humor. There was also the secrecy of it, the idea that they were both of them hiding all of this from Kaye, and that she wasn't even admitting to being Kaye's wife. Intriguing. Where it was all heading was not something Levin worried about. More to the point, the talking gray parrot had little to tell so far. He needed more to offer her, more sheets in his file folder, even if they added up to nothing.

The university art department was the logical place to go for collecting information about Weiss. There were colleagues to talk to, students, secretaries, perhaps others. He himself had been a history student here, and then a sometime visitor, though not in ages. It felt surprisingly congenial to him, being back on the hilltop campus. Things had changed, but all seemed as removed and tranquil as ever. The exploding back-pack that had demolished the cafeteria was so far an exception. Jews and Arabs, sensible ones, studied here together. The campus up on Mt. Scopus seemed a secure place to be, with thick walls built to resemble the Old City walls, walls being emotionally so comforting. He had met Miriam here, when they were students. Here they had studied, slept and dreamt together. On an impulse, or putting off his mission, he climbed the heights to the upper reaches of the amphitheatre and looked out over the still-blank page of the brown Judean Hills. A sweet nostalgia swept over him, despite himself. He felt sentimental, even about Miriam—even about them—up here in an empty amphitheatre. Life was hazardous. You never knew about yourself. You never knew.

Weiss's friend. Everywhere he went, the art history department, the library, the central office, Levin presented himself as the bereaved friend, trying to understand the tragedy of Weiss's death. In his mind he saw a sweaty, post-coital Weiss igniting a cigarette, or a brutish Weiss lunging with his walking stick. But on his rounds he put all that aside, not difficult, since generally he listened while people spoke well of the dead. Colleagues remembered a dedicated scholar, on the moody side perhaps, a very private sort of man. Yes, he talked vaguely about moving to America, but who didn't, after one terrorist act or another. He was well-liked by his students, as far as anyone knew. A few anecdotes recalled some lighter moments from his life. He had no family here. He had always lived alone. No, he wasn't romantically attached, they observed, but who could definitely say? Me. I can say, thought Levin. I know more about him than you do. He thanked them all politely. It was a predictable waste of time.

He never spoke to any of Weiss's students. The closest he came was a visit to the rebuilt cafeteria, where he contemplated asking around for anyone who had known Professor Weiss. The big room was crowded and shrill with youthful voices. Levin sat over a cup of coffee, feeling subdued and mute. Young girls everywhere. Girls eating, talking, quiet, laughing, a hive of girls behind those thick walls, like fairies under a rock. Lately, it was hard to tell when they were pretty or only young or if it mattered. Eyeing them, he felt very much the wolf in sheep's clothing. No—not the wolf. A lamb in sheep's clothing. Ever the shy and unsure lamb.

A student sat down next to Levin, a male student. He had a cup of coffee too.

"I've been watching you," said the student. "You look like a wise man. I'm looking for an advisor."

"You're mistaken. I'm afraid I don't teach here," said Levin.

"That's beside the point. But all right. For the sake of argument I'll let it go." The student extended his hand. "Schidlov. I'm one of the Russians. That's why I probably look like an American to you. But in reality I'm straight out of Dostoyevsky."

Levin shook his hand. Meanwhile Schidlov kept talking.

"You know those scenes in Dostoyevsky where a total stranger sits down and tells you the story of his life? That's remarkably like me. I was born in Moscow. My parents brought me to Israel for a better life. Also, there was no place else to go. So I went to school, I grew up, and here I am, as you see me. That's basically my story."

"Short and sweet," said Levin.

"Sweet? I wouldn't say so. Neither would you, if you knew my parents. They're stubborn, selfish and greedy. Even in Israel they stick out as Jews. Back in Russia, they would stick out as Russian peasants. Stubborn, selfish and greedy, religious Jews and religious peasants, the same basic type. Are you religious?"

"No, I'm not."

"They're both very religious, if you count superstitious. They even have Dostoyevsky's peasants' hands, big strong hands, with big soft thumbs. But it's a sham, having those thumbs and the rest. I learned that early in life. That's why I became an atheist. I have no belief in God whatsoever. I'm way above that. But guess what? At the very same time, I can imagine that God is patting me on the head and telling me, 'You atheists, you're the only ones I have any respect for. You're the only ones who know how to think. So don't mind me. Keep it up.'"

"That's very interesting," Levin said truthfully. "You're a very interesting young man."

"Will you be my advisor?"

"I thought we settled that. Aside from the fact that I don't teach here, you don't even know me."

"So? Do you think I haven't considered that? I was hoping you understood me better."

"Were you here when the bomb went off, that day in the cafeteria?"

"No. I was far from here."

"I'm glad you were," said Levin. "I'm glad you were."

Levin didn't get up. Yet he had nothing more to say. Why stay? It grew very awkward.

"I should go now. I have things to do. Thank you for your company. I wish you luck."

"If you change your mind I'm always here about now."

Leave Jerusalem . . . that's my advice, if you want it. Leave now . . . go far away. Run to Paris. I would. Your parents made a bad mistake. You don't belong here. You never will.

Levin uttered none of this, not a word. He wanted to. It was wise advice. But it seemed too cynical even for him, a cynic. Jerusalem a mistake? Israel a mistake, the historic homeland? For that was what he meant, deep down. How many other Jews shared his fear these days, his secret fear of the history they had made?

He reached out and squeezed Schidlov's shoulder, a gesture of both hopefulness and very sad regret, and hurried from the noisy cafeteria.

11

He placed the ad in the *Holy Land Times*: "Talking gray parrot for sale."

His normally silent phone began to ring. The first calls and the last were not from Deborah Kaye.

Parrots were in some demand in Jerusalem. Maybe all pets were, for the solace they brought; maybe people living in such uncertainty craved the special comfort of a repetitive talking bird. His callers barely let him speak, they were so flush with questions: How old was the parrot, what sex, what size, was it a pure-bred African gray? His stock answer, when they finally let him give it, was that unfortunately they were too late, the parrot had been sold. He had no other parrot, there was only the one. He got no joy out of disappointing them. They never guessed how much their voices disappointed him.

But Deborah Kaye—being herself—asked no questions.

"Hello, Levin. It's me. I've been waiting for you. Over on Graetz Street, near the center, there's a jewelry store, Artinian's. You can't miss it. At one o'clock today, I'll meet you there."

No frills, no nonsense. Yet Levin dressed with unusual care, putting on his blue blazer, tan slacks, a French blue shirt and a Panama hat. When he looked at the result in the mirror, he saw what a waste of time it was. Mostly, he reminded himself of those old dowagers who get their hair set, put on fine gowns and jewels, only to be seen for exactly what they are, old ladies in disguise. A thick skin was your best hope, after a while. A tough old hide.

And good lungs. He wasn't a health nut, but he had stopped smoking cigarettes years ago. Graetz Street was a long walk for him, but he arrived there in fine shape, barely wheezing. This was the so-called German colony, the neighborhood where German Jews had settled after fleeing the Nazis. The broad street was tree-lined, gracious, very fashionable, and looked more like the middle of Europe than the Middle East. Weiss's family had been German. He might have lived here, in a shabby garret with a fancy address. The philandering art historian might had led a life like that.

"A jewelry store, Artinian's. You can't miss it," she had said. True enough. But of course he knew the place before he sighted it, having waited across the street that day, keeping his tawdry vigil for twenty slow minutes. The time was just one o'clock. She wasn't standing outside. She must be inside.

She was—there in her big-brimmed hat, standing at the counter, her back to him. A small dark man behind the counter glanced past her and called to Levin: "Good-day."

"Good-day," responded Levin.

He thought that her turning around was one of the memorable moments of his life. That was how softened-up his tough hide was. She looked at him and he felt thrilled, just thrilled, without trusting her, without even knowing her. He touched the brim of his Panama. He was terribly glad that he had come dressed-up.

"I'm glad you came," said Deborah Kaye.

She didn't bother about Artinian, if he was the dark man behind the counter. As Levin started to speak, she told him, "Not here. There's another room."

The back room. The hypothetical back room with the sneaky back door. Here it was, a reality, solid proof, though proof of what, he still couldn't absolutely say. Deborah Kaye took off her hat. Levin removed his. He knew one thing for certain: this was no jeweler's workroom. There were a sofa, two comfortable chairs, a coffee table, a small refrigerator.

"Artinian," Deborah Kaye explained. "He's an activist. They hold meetings here."

An activist? Levin wondered what that might be. A peace activist? An Armenian activist? A hot diamonds activist? He took it for granted that she was lying. She seemed to lie without thinking about it, without even hearing the words on her tongue. There was a sort of absolution about it, like snow that fell without a trace.

They sat down, she on the sofa, he on a chair, his hat on his knee, leaning forward. "I wish I had something important to tell you. There are still possibilities, I'm not done, but I have nothing solid, not yet. I went where you said. I saw people at the university, people who knew him. They were all devastated. They all spoke so well of him. I wish they could have known something more." She was listening very closely. He was ashamed of himself for making her so attentive, basically, to nothing. "The police weren't too much help either, not in Jerusalem or in Jaffa"—deliberately giving the false impression that he had gone up to Jaffa for her. "They're still investigating. They couldn't convince me that it was the random act of a terrorist. I went and questioned the vendor at the bazaar, the Arab you told me threatened him. It was a useful conversation. He could be a suspect. He had a motive. I'm leaving that open for now." He hated giving her hope where there was none to give, but there was no stopping himself. "I have my old friends in the security service. They have all sorts of inside information. I can take the whole problem to them."

"I miss him."

It was remarkable, how that wounded Levin, as if in helping her, supporting her, he had rights. They were pretty quick rights; yet he felt them. That small sofa must have been where she made love with Weiss for most of twenty minutes.

"I can understand your loss," he told her. "You must have been terribly fond of your cousin."

"Karl? Karl was a baby."

What kind of an answer was that? Was her bogus cousin too childish to be a real lover? Or was a childish lover exactly what she wanted? Either way, she had a very different view of Weiss than he did. Women loved to make babies of men. The male was incurably immature, a suckling of one age of development or another. Any woman could dismiss a man that way. And it would usually sound like the truth.

Levin put on his hat. It wasn't to say good-bye. It was to go and sit beside her on the sofa, as if the farewell gesture freed him for anything he might do. He put his arm around her; with his finger he lifted her chin. "I'll keep trying. Give me more time. Sooner or later, people start talking. If he can be found, I'll find him."

"At the university," said Deborah Kaye quietly, "there's a teacher, a professor. He's in the math department. His name is Kaye. You didn't see him, did you?"

"No. Why would I?"

"He knew Karl. They used to be friends. He might know something."

"Like what?"

"I couldn't say. But Karl talked about him sometimes. Something happened between them."

"You think he could be involved in Karl's murder?"

She didn't speak. She let it rest there, sitting passively, with Levin's arm around her. Then she said to him, "I should go." She motioned to the back door. "We can leave from here."

It was understood that they would meet again. But it wouldn't be by way of a talking parrot this time. She was perfectly direct. "Suppose I telephone you. Say, in a week."

She had dark eyes, full lips that were flattened out, as if sculpted, dark eyebrows, a strong nose, shining dark hair. Her skin, beyond tanned, was born tawny. It was an old world face—a Semite face—harking back to Asia, and then to Europe for whole centuries, and now back to Asia, all the way back to this place, Jerusalem, again, perhaps a place no longer home.

Did he want her? Simple wanting, somehow, didn't apply. After the doom of her marriage, and the death of her lover, and with all of her baggage and lies, Levin felt he had inherited her.

12

A week. He had a week to find something that would keep him close to Deborah Kaye.

There was no point in covering old ground. Nor could he sit at home and simply make things up. Aside from the deceit, she would catch him at it and start to see him as he was, an old secret eye with secret intentions. That was the problem: to be perceived by her on one level while circling her down on another, drawing closer to her all the time.

Needing something new, it might be useful to drop in at the security service, as he had already told her he would do. That was the reason she had approached him in the first place, when she heard about his official expertise. Kaye, for all his slyness, hadn't exaggerated that. The security service had a file on almost everyone who had a face; they were a warehouse of information. It wasn't impossible that an item related to Weiss could be found.

But it would be awkward, revisiting the old place. He knew he would have to be more sociable than he felt, and there was something embarrassing about going back, interrupting men at work, reimposing yourself, as if you were celebrating a reunion of one. The old corridors, they never changed, with their familiar bends and echoes of long-gone conversations. He knew of retired men who couldn't bring themselves to walk past the buildings they had spent their active lives in, who would instead detour blocks out of their way.

With him, the reluctance came from something more. Levin

knew it when he stood across the street from the staid old government building with its sinister inner life, like Death dressed in a business suit. Behind its walls, old comrades were working in a struggle that Levin had less and less faith in, and that even some still inside had lost their stomach for. It wasn't complicated. Get the Arabs, get them out, as many of them as possible. The Arabs had a similar plan. Get the Jews out, all of them if possible. There was no solution, only the same old excruciating puzzle. The genius who said that two bodies couldn't occupy the same space at the same time wasn't thinking of the Holy Land, the divine real estate, where the same towns owned both Hebraic and Arabic names. And not only were these living Jews and Arabs here. Their dead ancestors all seemed present too, more bodies to be tripped over, or kicked aside, while God and Allah sorted out the rightful owners.

No; he didn't cross the street and re-enter the shadowy building. He went home, glad that he was done with his public service, his duty, and the struggle. He took out his relic of a briefcase and put a few folders into it, folders he marked "Weiss, Karl, Background," and "Current Info," and "Future Possibilities," and that he dignified with sheets of broadly scribbled notes. He had a dossier he could show her, with the impression that it came from secret police files, private nameless sources, even from the security service, whose facade he had stood and looked at. It was a joke. He went to the mirror and looked at his own facade, plain, staid, deceiving, dressed in street clothes, just like the old gray building.

He had a fresh idea, one that would bring him into contact with something real. He phoned the university for Weiss's former address. They gave it to him, not mentioning that the addressee had somehow or other moved on. Bureaucracies often functioned in that absent-minded way, an excellent thing, because he also had his expired security service credentials, giving him entry to nothing, but good enough to fool the average citizen when glimpsed in a window of his wallet. He wasn't the Law exactly. Helping Deborah Kaye find justice, he was a notch above the Law, or just below it, anyway in the vicinity.

Weiss hadn't resided in the German colony after all, but on the other side of Jerusalem in the Old City, in a Jewish neighborhood smack up against the Muslim quarter. Within hearing were those sinuous calls to prayer; within sight, shop signs in Arabic, women in abayas, Arab urchins playing in the street, minarets standing over an otherwise kneeling landscape. Weiss the art lover may have found it picturesque. Either that, or he was very poorly paid. Life was much cheaper here, cheek-by-jowl with the Arabs. His former apartment house was fairly barren, of stucco the color of sand, with narrow windows, with a few wishful plants out on the ledges. Weiss had rented a room in someone else's apartment. Levin had the number, on the topmost floor. Naturally, the elevator was out of service. As he mounted, he wondered, not quite believing it: had Deborah Kaye climbed these creaking stairs for sex, love, art appreciation or anything else, her heart quickening as she drew closer to Weiss?

A woman holding a baby in her arms came to the door. "Hello," said Levin and he thrust out his credentials. "I'm sorry to bother you. I'm with the national security service. I'd like to talk to you about Professor Weiss."

"Oh God. You'll take his things away?"

"What things?"

"All of it. The clothes, the books, everything."

"I'm sorry. That's actually not my department. But I know the right people to ask. I'll make a note of it. May I come in?"

He simply walked past her, into the living room. She followed after him, holding the wide-awake baby. "I need the money. I'm not working. I need to rent out the room."

"Of course you do. I understand. And so you shall, rest assured. May I sit down?"

He was already sitting. He regretted walking over her, but he figured this was the fastest way to get it done and leave her alone.

She sat down opposite him, she and the baby. Everything in the room was shabby, the furniture, the lace curtains, the old paint on the walls, shabby but neat and terribly clean, as if one could scrub something like newness back into them. She must have been a good landlady to Weiss. For extra money, she probably did his laundry. But Levin decided he couldn't go into that, the tales told by dirty human wash.

"I assume the police have been here," he said.

She shook her head. She wasn't saying no. It was the same weary complaint as before. "I told them too—take his things away, I need the room. But no one ever came back."

He took out a pen and pad and jotted down a note, presumably about removing Weiss's possessions. "Everyone sympathizes with you," he said gently. "We in the security service have seen more than enough of human pain and suffering. That's why we're determined to solve this crime. We believe it was the work of a terrorist, a brutal, random act. But there are still some troubling details, some loose ends we're working on."

What loose ends? He was glad she didn't ask. Her dimmed eyes on the baby, she didn't even seem to be listening to him. "I know this is difficult for you. Professor Weiss's death must have been a terrible shock, your boarder, a man you saw every day, perhaps your friend. That's why you're so important to us, if we're to bring his murderer to justice. During his stay here, did he ever talk about a person or persons who might have a motive to kill him, something involving money, politics, a personal relationship, something like that?"

With her thumb she wiped the baby's mouth. "I can't help you. I didn't know him. He paid his rent. We almost never spoke."

"Perhaps someone else here, perhaps your husband, used to talk to him?"

"I have no husband. My husband was taken from me."

Taken from her? By what or whom? Illness, the war, another woman? Just the phraseology suggested a disturbed mind to Levin, or some kind of religious mania.

"I'm very sorry. These are unbelievable, incredible days. I won't intrude on you much longer. But I have to ask. Can you recall any visitors Professor Weiss might have had?"

She didn't answer at all this time. Why not? What did she remember? Levin dared to think she was hiding something behind all her complaining. Then, as he watched, with a quick flip she pulled her breast out of her loose dress, lifted the baby's head and began to nurse.

Levin looked away. Feeding time. Private time—more private than he needed. True, he could have quietly excused himself and gone away. But he didn't. He still had his list of questions for his file: Weiss's visitors, his living mode, his habits. That was one reason he stayed fixed in his chair. For another, he was immobilized by what he wouldn't watch—almost too embarrassed by it to move. Sucking sounds of hunger and thirst told him the feeding was still going on. It was hard to comprehend. He knew that women from older cultures nursed their babies in public. But so did brazen modern ones. So which was she?

Or was there something very dark at work, that she herself was only dimly conscious of? Was this an act of aggression on her part, an act of defiance, the only kind she had? She was desperate and no one would help her. She was fed up with all of them, the police, her country, Weiss's things, Weiss himself by now. Why not shove her bare, drained tit in Levin's face?

Why not. Her husband had been taken, a baby had been left; probably the elevator was always out of service. Levin was sorry for her, somehow irritated but sorry too. He took out his wallet and waved some money at her, still averting his face.

"I'm sure that Professor Weiss would want you to have this. Wherever he is, he wouldn't want to cause you any more trouble than he has."

Nothing happened for a minute. Then the sucking stopped. Levin felt the bills lifted from his fingers. She was standing over him, all covered up again, when he turned and looked.

"Before I go, before I make my report to my people, can I take a look at his room?"

She led him to it, through a dim hallway, rocking the sleeping baby. Weiss's room resembled Weiss, bookish, messy, overstuffed. There were too many art books, art portfolios, statuettes, pictures crowding the walls. More books were crammed under the big bed. Weiss's walking stick lay like a ghost on top of the made-up bed. Levin asked to see the closet and bureau drawers, but she said no. "You're not the police. I'm all alone here. Suppose you took something. I don't want anyone blaming me."

"I understand."

He didn't, but he didn't expect reasonableness from her. He didn't expect that Weiss's pants or underwear would tell him anything important either. All in all, he had bothered an unfortunate woman without the slightest advance in the case. She had nothing to do with Weiss's death, terrorists, God and Allah, Deborah Kaye or Kaye. She was innocent of all that.

He felt ashamed of himself. His shame made him soft, sentimental. She stood at the front door, silently waiting for him to leave. There they were, she and her baby—mother and child—the smallest of families. People talked about the Big Picture. The Big Picture was vast, sweeping, significant. The little picture was the little life, the person, counting for something but not much. But look inside it and you had a big picture again, a woman and her fate, a human life with its own light, taking in the vastness with its own two eyes.

She caught him by the sleeve as he was exiting. But she had nothing new to say. It was the same old story to the end.

"Don't forget. Please—please send somebody to take away his things."

13

And now Kaye.

It had to be done. He could have fooled Deborah Kaye into believing that he had gone to the university and interviewed Professor Kaye as she suggested. How would she discover that he hadn't, since Kaye would never enlighten her on the subject.

But he couldn't deceive her, not about something so vital. She of course could twist the truth and he accepted it. He had done more thinking about Deborah Kaye lying. It had a lot to do with her position as a woman, forced to defend herself against predators like Weiss and Kaye, meaning the great bulk of men, himself included. To protect themselves, women were entitled to all means of deception, the weaponry of slaves, because despite their advances, women were still a slave class. They were vulnerable. They were over-burdened. He felt sorry for women all over the world. Anyway, that was his feeling today, after his experience with Weiss's landlady, the desperate woman alone with her baby. She had tenderized him, a small chunk of him, like a butcher working on a steak.

He had begun to daydream about Deborah Kaye. Who would have foreseen, when he was fifteen, that he would still be daydreaming about females at sixty? These elder dreams stretched reality a bit. He was untiring and potent, fully up to the demands of an ever desiring Deborah Kaye. Actually, her body played a lesser role than her face. He had seen precious little of her body, and even daydreams had their limits. Her face fascinated him. He had seen it coming toward him and up close, bare-headed and with a big-brimmed hat, film-star glamorous and smeared with mud. Like a Mona Lisa she was consumed by her face, and it was all his fantasies required: the brown eyes, the flat-lipped, sculpted mouth, her mouth and eyes widening as he pleasured her.

To see Kaye now, under the altered circumstances, repelled Levin. Do not covet thy neighbor's wife. It was no help to him that Kaye was not even a friend, or a man he liked, or that Weiss had more than cleared the way to coveting. How did you confront a man whose wife you licked and ravished in your dreams—not only confront him, but probe him, and try to make a murder suspect out of him, which Levin still found hard to believe.

But it had to be done. He picked up his phone and called Kaye. In fact, he had to call him persistently, before he got Kaye in person, so as not to leave any sort of message. Rationally or not, he felt a need to be cautious.

"I have to see you right away," Levin told him. "You may be in trouble. But I'm not coming to your office. It'll have to be somewhere else."

"Why? What's happened? Why not here?"

Kaye was rattled, a good first step. Levin decided to scare him more. "I was thinking of a public place, with a big crowd, where we wouldn't be noticed. Like the Central Bus Station."

"Are you mad? No bus stations—no buses. No bomb sites."

"East Jerusalem then, Arab territory. I think they're less likely to follow you there. Take down these directions. It's a cafe."

"Who won't follow me?"

"Write this down." He gave Kaye very roundabout directions. "To be on the safe side. And take an Arab taxi. That's safer too."

He allowed plenty of time for Kaye to arrive there first, to sit and wait and worry, before he rode up in his own Arab taxi.

He found Kaye at a table in the back, as far from the sidewalk as one could get.

"I'm glad you didn't sit in the open," Levin told him, sliding into a chair.

"Do you think I'm an idiot? What took you so long? What's this all about?"

"Let's order something first. We'll look more natural."

They ordered Turkish coffee. Then Levin called the waiter back and asked for a serving of dates, a particular kind, which he discussed in Arabic with the waiter, one more prevarication to unsettle Kaye. He was trying to frame the conditions of an interrogation, in so far as he could. Separate the suspect from familiar surroundings. Put him in an uncomfortable, hostile environment—an Arab cafe would do. Control the tempo. Introduce surprises. Keep the suspect off-balance.

Levin looked down at the table, enforcing silence, as the waiter set down the coffee and dates and left.

"I'm taking a risk," he said. "That may explain something. I shouldn't be seen with you."

Kaye stared back at him. "What do you mean by that?"

"Calm down. Drink your coffee. I came to warn you. The authorities think you may have murdered Karl Weiss."

"Murdered Weiss? I can't believe it. They can't have any evidence of that."

"We're not talking about evidence, not yet. We're talking about suspicion. They found your wife's letters in Weiss's room. They know about their affair. I happened to be visiting my old office, which I do occasionally, and they were all talking about it. You're a well-known figure. An eminent professor. That makes it an irresistible story. They think the love triangle points to you."

"Tell me why the security service would be interested in this."

"They were investigating it as a terrorist act. It concerns them if it isn't."

"Well, it's a total fabrication. Pure gossip. I can tell you that Deborah never writes letters."

"I only know what I heard."

Levin selected a date. He chewed it with open pleasure, rudely, in Kaye's face. He realized he was having a fine time, going to work on Kaye.

"It's a lucky thing you're hearing this from me," he said. "Someone else might think you looked frightened."

"To be perfectly honest, when you called I thought it had something to do with the university." Kaye looked more weary than afraid now. "Academia politics. It's as cutthroat as you get. Spying is an option; so is blackmail. People will stoop to anything."

Was Kaye being honest? And what would someone blackmail him for? With no idea, Levin stuck to his line of questioning. "Now that you know the facts, what do you think?"

"About me killing Weiss?"

"Yes."

"It's a possibility. I thought about it enough. A crime of passion. They could have stumbled on something."

"Are you implying that you actually murdered Weiss?"

"I'm saying I had the motive. You should know that. You supplied it. You clinched it for me."

"I don't believe you murdered Karl Weiss."

"That floating scum? Why wouldn't I?" Kaye stared down at his hands. "All right. Say I can't do it myself. But I dearly want it done. Say I make inquiries in certain quarters, looking for a killer for hire, Arab, Jew, Christian, there's a healthy assortment here. Say I get hold of some Jew out of Russia, a gangster type, that's the likeliest. I hire him to get in a car that day, follow Weiss's car, stop him on the road, and blow his brains out. Let's say I've come along too, to see the show. I suddenly step out of the car. I call out. My happy face is the last face the swine sees before his head is blown away. Ripped off—

isn't that what the paper said? It's a real beheading. The neck knows it first. The head looks surprised, and then the rest of him tumbles down too. I stand there. Can you imagine my satisfaction? Can you picture it?"

Kaye picked up a date, tasted it, and swallowed the rest. "You were right. These are delicious."

Levin could picture Kaye's satisfaction. Vividly. Kaye was being Kaye. He described Weiss dying as graphically and zestfully as he had described Weiss and his wife having sex. Kaye had demons. And when a man had demons driving him on, who could separate them from reality? Yet Levin still couldn't believe that the man in front of him had murdered Weiss.

"This isn't mathematics," Levin said. "You don't sit around throwing out hypotheses. This is arithmetic. One plus one. You ought to watch what you say—they'll add it up. They're thinking about you, even if they don't have the evidence. Be very careful."

"I thought I was being careful. I'm working under the assumption that this little pleasantry is between you and me. Am I wrong?"

Levin shook his head. Let Kaye make of that naysaying whatever he would. Neither of them much trusted the other. It was a standoff. The interrogation was over, Levin had no further questions. But he had enjoyed seeing Kaye rattled, the controlled man out of control. Interrogating someone could do that to you, powerfully incite you, make you quite sadistic. He had experienced the temptation before. It was all the more tempting when the someone was the husband of the woman you dreamed about.

They made no plans to meet again. Why would they? Kaye would go back to Deborah Kaye and Levin would go home and wait for her call. They went their separate ways, in separate Arab taxis. It was always a pleasure to see the last of Kaye.

Levin made notes of the meeting in Weiss's dossier, and waited for his phone to ring. He rarely left the apartment. It wasn't yet a week, but she could call him sooner, couldn't she? He stocked up on sandwiches so he wouldn't be out eating and miss her call. Pathetic. It was possible she wouldn't even call. She'd meet someone else and her life would take a completely different turn. She was like that. Another fish was slowing down. His tank was like a clock running down, a heart giving out. Pay attention to fishes. Fishes were mystical things—fishes and loaves. Fishes were also sexual. Immersion and slime.

He was really in a bad way.

14

Another bad omen: on one of his few quick trips outside, he ran into Miriam.

The ghost of blisses past. She was walking straight toward him, so there was no avoiding her. Plus, she was in high spirits, meaning a lot better than his. The two of them were still competing but in a different way. Which of them felt greater happiness and more relief?

Levin put on his best face, sheer performance. So it occurred to him that maybe she was feigning cheeriness too. She looked slightly different. He realized that she had changed her hairdo. Her gray hair was now in braids, with the braids arranged on top of her head. What to think about a woman who braided her gray hair? Levin thought this: The gray bespoke her naturalness. The braids her youthfulness. It was the hairdo of an idealist, a woman who kept hope alive, and it beautifully suited her. But Levin could only imagine the drudgery of making love to a gray-braided woman.

Fortunately, it wasn't a personal conversation. She talked about the situation, the never-ending struggle between the Jews and Arabs. She saw signs of change. Some Jewish pilots were refusing to bomb the Arabs. The peace movement was winning new allies. Levin had no quarrel with this. They both shared the same liberal-minded view. But he was more and more a sideline observer, a fan of peace, while she was down on the playing field, still swinging away. She organized protests, marched in rallies, wrote impassioned articles. In the latest one, which he had read, which she now repeated for him, she accused the government of the unforgivable, acting like fascists. She hadn't called them Nazis, the unmentionable, but the comparison was there, the occupying, oppressing Jews as the new master race. The moral turnabout astounded her. What did the Jews stand for after their long, suffering history, if not for justice?

Levin was itching to get home to his phone. He kept mum, not wanting to encourage her. Once she actually touched him, grasping his arm in her fervor. She was unaware of the shock of this, their first physical contact since their divorce. But to Levin it was the pivotal point of the encounter, whatever crisis she thought she was telling him about. He simply turned and tore himself away. He had been absent from his apartment for thirty minutes when he rushed back in as if his phone were ringing, which it was not.

Next morning, while he was drinking his coffee, stalling over the cold second cup, Deborah Kaye finally called. Her first words were not words that Levin wanted to hear.

"Did you find out anything? Is there any point in our meeting again?"

He was floored. "Absolutely there's a point. It's been a whole week. I've been very busy. I have a number of developments for you."

"I see. Hold on."

Where did she go? Was she at home with Kaye and being careful? Or was it her technique, to leave people dangling, hanging on? Levin sat and held—he had no choice.

She was back. "All right. Where do we meet?"

Here, my apartment, he wished he could say. Or failing that, someplace with atmosphere, like the King David Hotel. But he knew he had to be discreet, as discreet as if they were lovers.

"I thought of that. The Tower of David Museum. Do you

know it? It's out-of-the-way, quiet, ideal for us. Can you be there at ten tomorrow morning?"

"Of course."

"Meet me inside, in the old part, the tower."

He wore the same ensemble that he had worn to the Armenian's: the sports jacket, the French blue shirt, the Panama hat. It was his snappiest outfit, and he doubted she would remember any of it. Despite his best intentions, he was too early and arrived first. When she walked into the old ruin, looking around for him, he remembered the day he had imagined he saw her here. Actually seeing her seemed beyond belief.

"Have you been here before?" she asked him.

"A few times. And you?"

"My first."

"King David was never here either. In fact, according to some scholars, there may never have been a King David."

"You can't kid me," said Deborah Kaye. "I've had martinis in his hotel."

Levin laughed. He gave her credit for trying to lighten things up. It was a strained moment. She was really interested in his briefcase, dangling from his hand, and what it might contain about Weiss.

He took her to a bench. This morning, no other visitors were there. High craggy walls rose around them. With no roof—the sky was the roof—the billowy clouds had a biblical nearness.

Levin took out his batch of folders and talked his way through each of them. His notes from the security service, though made-up, were probably accurate, stating that Weiss's death was under investigation, with no solid leads, and presumably the work of an Arab terrorist.

"You already know about my session with the threatening Arab at the bazaar. I still haven't ruled him out."

"Did you see that professor at the university? Professor Kaye?"

"I'll get to that. I also did something else. I paid a visit to your cousin's room."

He didn't know what he expected. Fresh grief, sadness, tender recollection. That was the main reason he mentioned it, to extract some emotion from her, to satisfy his curiosity.

"You were in Karl's room."

That was all she said. You could read anything into it, that she resented Levin's going there, that she appreciated his going there. Levin said impassively, "I can't say I learned anything, beyond the fact that he lived so near the Arab quarter, whatever that could mean. His books and clothes are still there, by the way, if you want to pack them up."

"I haven't been able to go there . . . I'll try to send someone."

That left Kaye, Professor Kaye, the folder she was waiting for. Levin started cautiously. "I went to see Professor Kaye, as you suggested. It was a lengthy interview. I found him, frankly, a little odd. He's a clever man, but something—" Levin searched for the appropriate words—"something of a cold fish." Deborah Kaye said nothing. So Levin proceeded: "Exceptionally cold, I would say. He's one of those men with a controlling nature, an obsessiveness. He's not what you would call forgiving. He could decide to get rid of someone, then do it or have it done. I remembered what you told me about him. Based on my own experience, I decided to confront him outright, shake him up a bit, and I believe it worked. I brought up Karl, his violent death. Kaye admitted to me that he hated your cousin and had a good reason for wanting him dead. A reason. That's called a motive. Kaye wouldn't tell me what it was. Can you?"

"I have no idea. I only know what Karl told me. That they didn't get along."

"Do you know if Kaye is having problems at the university, with people in his department? He seemed extremely concerned about that."

"How would I know anything about his problems? I don't see why it would change anything. I think you were right when you talked about him. Clever. Cold. Obsessed. That sounds like the man Karl knew."

She was pointing to her husband as a cold-blooded killer. He was pointing to the same husband as a cold-blooded mate. Both of them were bent on saying what they wanted the other to believe.

"I'm not finished with Professor Kaye," he told her. "There's something very wrong about him. There may be more to this whole matter than we think."

He was looking into her eyes—looking to look, to be precise. He wished he dared to be more open with her, more explicit. But it was impossible, with the uncertain sense Levin had of himself.

She stood up. "I have to go. Thank you for everything you're doing. As the song says, we'll meet again. I like your hat. I liked it the last time too."

"Would you like to look around the museum? As long as we're here?"

"I don't think so . . . You're an interesting man. The security service, state secrets, all that. Your manner. There must be a lot you don't talk about."

"There is."

"You'll want to sleep with me, won't you?"

Levin was speechless. Almost. "Why are you putting it in the future?"

She half-smiled and touched Levin on the shoulder. "You might get to. But I wonder what you'd think," and she paused, "if I told you it wouldn't mean that much to me."

And he watched her cross the floor of the old ruin, indifferent to it, worlds away from the ancient walls and the biblical sky, her high heels clicking.

It wouldn't mean that much to me. He didn't know what to

make of her. She wasn't bluffing. She wasn't boasting. Why tell him such a thing? To shock him? She had certainly accomplished that. Bravo—he had real reason to be optimistic, if she kept on wanting to shock him.

But she was also telling him a fact about herself. What fact? That she was casual about sleeping with men? That she was sexually independent, on an equal footing with men? That sex was purely a physical diversion to her? All well and good. But who could blame him for being a little troubled, a little disappointed in advance, if sleeping with him wouldn't mean all that much to her.

He sat for a good long time on a bench in the deserted Tower of David. Where else was he to go? Myth, memory, both died hard. She was here as much as David was.

15

The terrorist act.

The patient gunman. The zooming car bomber. The silent guy wearing the explosive vest. Levin, for better or worse, could see it from their point of view. They used what they had, the way anyone would. The terror was in the eye of the beholder, like you know what, like beauty, the creation of a perfect moment—all hell and heaven too. In Jerusalem, there was more than one facet, one face to terror.

He hadn't witnessed a terrorist act in a long while. This was wholly by chance, by never being at ground zero at zero hour. Enough times, he had been somewhere in the vicinity when a bomb went off, the blast followed by the choral sirens of ambulances and army trucks, the sight of those lunging through traffic, toward a rising shroud of smoke. When he could, he followed the sirens to the scene, because anyone not hurt could help. Smoke, screams and blood were a given. Sometimes you saw the twisted torso of a bus, sometimes the burnt remains of a building, and each of them told you what the bomb would do to flesh. Levin had often rushed to a terror scene, and he was aware of the daily threat. But he hadn't been right on the spot, not recently, until today.

The target was a restaurant at lunch time. The method was a parked bicycle with an explosive strapped under the seat. As terror went, it was small stuff, and not suicidal, which always lent its own sickening taste to the event.

Levin was having lunch in a restaurant right across the

street. He had a forkful of food in his hand. At the roar of the blast he and those near him dove to the floor. Then came the screams, the smell of smoke, the splintered glass, not here, but just across the street.

Some stayed down on the floor. Others like Levin dashed into the open to the stricken restaurant. Walls were still shaking. People were dazed. No one was dead and the injuries seemed minor. But blood, haze and hysteria were everywhere. It was midday in the center of the city. Both Jews and Arabs had been in the restaurant. Even hurt and dazed, they stayed apart, helping their own. Levin himself had automatically gone to the aid of the Jews.

There was another conclave of people here too. They had come from elsewhere, afterward, like him. They were unhurt, clear-headed, here to offer help, to offer it to everyone. They were American men and women—Christian evangelicals. That was easy to see. They all wore T-shirts with the message: "Walk with Jesus." They carried palm leaves, which they threw down. They were pilgrims of the sort he often saw in Jerusalem, walking the path to Golgotha, retracing the Stations of the Cross.

They moved like angels among the frightened and afflicted, Jews and Arabs alike. They had bottles of water, which they held to trembling lips. They seemed to know the ways of comfort. Neither Jew nor Arab, they were innocents in all of this. Comforting, innocent, and in T-shirts—what could be more open-hearted, more American?

"Armageddon—"

Levin heard the word, heard it murmured about, as if suppressed, whispered. He turned around. "Walk with Jesus" said their T-shirts. But their composed faces were unreadable, like a book closed up.

Armageddon. The end of the world. Judgment Day. The Second Coming. They were passionate believers. They had journeyed to Jerusalem at their peril and now they were being rewarded with this glimpse of the fiery future. At a disaster, Levin knew, people were flung into themselves but outward too. They were of two different states, here and not here. They thought of their children, their parents, their loved ones. These folks had a different horizon: eternity. They welcomed the end of the world. Armageddon. Was it closer? Was Christ closer? Beneath their composure, Levin sensed their excitement. They didn't flinch from the maze of dust and chaos, or from getting blood all over their T-shirts. He wondered if they would keep the bloody shirts as mementos of their trip. The most avid of tourists, they came to shop for Armageddon, and today they had found a touch of it, a foretelling. For them, it was a perfect moment: Terror had more than a single face in Jerusalem. Then their sights fell to earth, and the soldiers and medics came.

His loved ones.

Levin could count them on the fingers of one hand, and he could probably discount the little finger.

His mother and his father. His children, not often seen, studying and then working outside the country . . . The little finger was Deborah Kaye. Was she a loved one or not? Was she even temporarily beloved by him? Yes, at the instant of the bomb-blast he had thought of her. That almost unknown face was among the cherished others. Reflecting afterward, he wondered if she would miss him if he perished that day, and knew that of course she never would. This fact should have ended the matter. But then he asked himself, like a stupid adolescent, would he die for her? Would he risk death for her if she wouldn't even miss him? Possibly he would, he thought, if the threat were sudden, certain, and he acted out of instinct. But he might do the same for a total stranger, say an endangered child. To narrow the focus: would he kill for her? Murder a rival, in the murderous manner entertained by Kaye? Not very likely. Nearly impossible. But it was interesting, as it had been as a schoolboy, testing himself on the circles of his love.

He stopped by his mother's, a routine visit. She read him letters from the grandchildren, his children, not exactly new letters, but better than nothing. "They're better off where they are," she said of her grandchildren. "They should stay far away from here." He knew it broke her heart to say this, broke it in a couple of places, but she meant it: her precious Jewish grandchildren were better off not being in Jerusalem. "What do you say?" she asked Levin, not that she was asking for his opinion. She was reassuring herself that he was actually with her, sitting here.

Her radio was on louder when she was alone. Then it blared away, talking to her, scaring her, keeping her company. Now it was lower but still there, keeping her up-to-the-minute. She talked about the latest atrocity"—a bomb on a bicycle, where Jewish people were eating. You'll see. They'll be putting bombs in our baby carriages next." Levin was silent on the subject. He wasn't about to tell her that he had been so close to the bicycle bomb. He would never frighten her like that.

She made lunch for him. He stood in the kitchen as she cooked it. Then, not eating anything herself, she sat down with him. Levin ate everything in front of him, ate happily. As ridiculous as it was, he felt snug and safe here, with this tiny old woman who could be frightened by a radio, who was herself besieged here, locked in with her horrific Leningrad memories. She was his mother—as if to say it explained anything. Mother and child. It wasn't rational. It went beyond the human, not upward and mystical, the other way, animal. Animal instinct was the only way to describe it. That he also loved her was a wholly different matter. Levin kissed her affectionately when he left. Family wasn't the trap it once was, the set trap you escaped from time after time, after school holidays and such. Family got to be precious with aging. It was just something that came on naturally, like an old man's tears.

He didn't go back to his apartment. He stopped in a small park midway to home, and chose to sit down against the trunk of a tree, he who always sat on benches. Today, he preferred the ground. It made him feel young. The air was balmy and he fanned himself with his Panama hat. He had grown very fond of the hat, which had spent years on the shelf in the closet. Now they were inseparable, in the style of Humphrey Bogart and John Wayne and other old-timers, who wore the same hat in movie after movie. Stretched out under the tree, he rested his Panama on his knee and looked at it. What a sweet moment. And in Jerusalem. He closed his eyes. A man and his hat. Not a care in the world.

16

S he was born in Haifa, a cosmopolitan town, her father a doctor, her mother a pianist, or less grandly, a piano teacher. She had one sibling, an older sister; no record of any cousins whatever, on one side or the other. She went through the Haifa public schools near the top of her class and went to university in Tel Aviv, where she studied law, along with minoring in French, a good but not a high-achieving student. Briefly engaged to a fellow law student, but no wedding bells. No outside employment while a student. Summers unaccounted for, likely spent cloistered with the doctor and the pianist. After law school, worked briefly at a law firm. Quit, got married, and never practiced law again.

She was now forty-two. She had been married to Kaye for twelve years. Splendid wedding. No children. A luxury Jerusalem apartment. Their travels together included Germany, France, Spain, Cyprus, Cairo, usually coinciding with a mathematics conference of Kaye's. She was hospitalized twice, once for severe back pain, the second time—why this?—for exhaustion. Afterward, she worked briefly at same hospital as a volunteer. Then she went back to school, here in Jerusalem, taking courses in the history of law. That qualified her for the position she held now (that and Kaye's influence?), teaching one course, two hours per week, on the history of Western law, which sounded suspiciously like a dilettante softy, to Levin.

Hours had gone into his research. When necessary, he made use of former contacts to access a source: Municipal records.

Educational transcripts. College and law school alumni mailings. Newspaper files. Medical records. He found three photographs of her. The last was a magazine photo of her with other women of the university faculty, just a posed face in a back row. Then there was the newspaper photo that accompanied their wedding announcement, Kaye looking unalterably as he did now, Deborah youthful, her hair longer, smiling for the photographer. The earliest picture was with her law class. Here, her new-graduate gaze was direct, self-knowing, her sensuous lips not smiling for anyone.

She wouldn't have paid much attention to somebody like him back in the university, that striking a girl. She might have talked to him as they left a class, or borrowed his notes to study for an exam, but she would never have gone out on a date with him. He would never have had the nerve to ask. Yet last week she volunteered that she might sleep with him. Levin sat in the Tel Aviv newspaper office and looked at that early photograph for a long time. It made the trip to Tel Aviv worthwhile. He was tempted to steal that picture of her and take it with him. It was a vindication of the round, shy, lonely boy he had been, that this girl could want him now. It was a triumph.

Life had worn her down. He felt compelled to admit this, even though it rather spoiled the triumph. The years had caught up with her and made her attainable to him. That would also explain the entrance of Weiss into her life. Maybe to a degree it explained Kaye.

Now she was all over the map with men. Kaye was ten years older than she, Weiss a dozen years younger. Levin was in a different dimension entirely, being older by almost twenty years. She was all over the map, except for men her own age. Of course, he didn't know everything. There must have been additional men. Her broken engagement had been to a fellow student, probably in his twenties like her. He assumed it was she who broke it off. Perhaps she preferred another student, or a professor. From photo to photo, she obviously would never have had a problem attracting men. He couldn't begin to put himself in her place, swatting off men and their eyes from the minute she entered a room. A girl armed with her face and allure, going out into the world, unleashing male desire, what power that must bring. What fear, too, knowing how ready they were for her, more than, they and their zippers. And then, what boredom, surely, after a while. So much of inevitably the same. He must remember never to be boring to her. At his age, that seemed especially important. Also, it played to his strength, the gray man with the rainbow mind.

Why law school? It didn't fit. It was an easy way of postponing life, in most cases, and she apparently knew it. She quit on her first job and never went back to practicing. Did she marry the established Kaye in order to be free of work altogether? He couldn't presume that. To last twelve years, Deborah and Kaye had built some sort of life together, something binding, if strained and tortuous. Which of them hadn't wanted children, assuming they were able to have them? Probably neither one, he guessed. Kaye, the obsessed egoist, wouldn't share Deborah with anyone, and Deborah wasn't domestic, not even domesticated, as Kaye would find out. Severe back pain. Exhaustion . . . From over-strenuous sex? A cheap thought, and Levin knew it. Stress and nerves were more likely possibilities, or something anatomical. She was tautly made. The Dead Sea mud couldn't cover up her cheekbones. Her clipped speech sounded tense. Her tension, in a way, kept her young. Her discontent kept her going, like a current of electricity.

Now she was back to law, in a marginal way, teaching two hours a week, teaching the history of Western law to students who were probably as bored with the profession of law as she herself. She was more like them than they thought, unsure, just holding on, but not at the beginning—nearer the end.

If there was anything more to be gleaned from his research, Levin didn't know what it was. With all his information, he felt on more equal terms with her. He was pretty pleased with himself, the skilled old hand sifting the intelligence. He had given life to a full-blown woman whose soul and saliva he could taste. A good question was: Was it true?

"I know who you are."

He meant, "I know that you are married to Kaye."

Did he have the nerve to say it to her? Was it smart? The last thing he wanted was to scare her off, and she apparently felt safer keeping hidden. But people often had a secret wish to confess to the right interrogator. She might be glad to come clean as Kaye's wife. Levin might be moved to confess that he knew Kaye, and precisely how, and therefore all about Weiss. It could be a wonderful scene, filled with sincerity and pathos. And then what? Mere good friends for life? Levin really didn't care to risk that.

She didn't wait a week this time. Only six days passed, like Creation, before she phoned him again.

"I have a great idea," Levin said. "Let's meet for lunch at the King David Hotel."

"Why not David's Tower again? Or don't you think we belong in a museum?"

She was afraid she had insulted him. Of course she hadn't. He liked her coupling the two of them, in whatever way. But she added quickly:

"Forget I said that. I know a good place. It's a student hangout. We can have a very young lunch."

It was the cafe where she had sat at a table next to Weiss, ages ago it seemed, that day when both had moved on to the Armenian jeweler's back room. With a joy that was absurd, Levin saw her sitting at the very same table, here in Jerusalem, where history loved to repeat itself. The place was brimming

with youth, eating hungrily and fearless enough to sit anywhere, including the wide-open sidewalk tables. Here in the
back, they ordered burgers. The cuisine fit the clientele: thin,
fast and fried. Teenage girls were there, as full of life as ever,
but they were no distraction to Levin. He only hoped that
Deborah Kaye wasn't remembering Weiss.

He hoped she wasn't thinking about Weiss's killer either,
waiting to ask him for news. He had none, although he came
prepared to bluff: He was still digging for information about
Professor Kaye. He was still seeking out unknown visitors to
Weiss's room. Based on art objects he had seen in that room,
he was looking into the murky antiquities trade, based in nearby Arab Jerusalem. Truthfully, the only fresh happening in his
life since he last saw her was the bicycle bombing, totally off
the subject. But that was what Levin started talking about.

"You may have read about it. It was a cafe-restaurant like
this one, but the terrace was enclosed by glass, which naturally
made everything worse. That's the cunning, if you will, behind
these bombings. First there's the blast. Then comes the shattered glass, the shrapnel, the nails and razors and so on, the
most terrifying part. In this case, the bomb was small and simple, hidden under a bicycle seat. You wonder if the terrorist
gave any thought to riding the bicycle inside and exploding it
under himself. These are fantastically daring if totally irrational
people. I was in a restaurant across the street. We heard a blast.
The next moment we were ducking flying glass. But the blood-
shed was pretty minimal, even in the target cafe. Some of us
ran across to help them. Big bomb or small, it's always a
hideous scene. Have you ever been anywhere close to a terrorist attack?"

Levin spoke matter-of-factly, almost impersonally. And as
he spoke, he realized that he was trying to impress her with his
professional experience, with his coolness under fire. He was
using the terror to romance her, and hoping that it worked.

"I don't know anything about that bomb. I don't follow the news," she said. "No, I've never been close to an attack. I've been lucky. I haven't been touched by the war. . .except for Karl, if he died that way. It really is a war, isn't it, whatever we call it. I don't know. I'm not political. I try not to think about it. I've never seen a terrorist. I don't know any Arabs. I don't know any religious Jews either, for that matter. Sometimes I don't know why I'm living here. Because I'm Jewish, I suppose. I can usually accept that as a reason, when I'm not scared to death. People like you, who fought to keep us here, we have a lot to thank you for.

"You would have liked my father," Deborah Kaye said with a smile. "Either that, or hated him. He was a strong man too. He was a doctor, methodical, very brilliant, and with a beard like Freud's. He even smoked cigars—a real stereotype. My mother was a different stereotype, a pianist, the dreamy, sensitive artist. I think that basically all people are stereotypes, don't you, with a few little quirks thrown in? At least, that's been my experience. I talk about my parents as if they're dead. They're very much alive. I just don't see them that much anymore. Did I tell you that I'm married? Or did I forget? We don't have any children. Promise me you won't ask why. It might be fun to guess. I was engaged to someone once, back in college. That was real fun. I should have stayed engaged forever, but dumb me, I up and graduated. I was a lawyer, would you believe that? I hated it—hated it. I have another job now, but I'm not telling you what it is. You'd know who I am. I mean, I am who I say, but there's more to it than that. I miss Karl. I hope you find him—I mean his murderer. Levin—say something. Shut me up. Please—I can't stop talking."

He touched her hand. "Quiet, be quiet. Calm down."

She shut her mouth in her own way. She leaned across the table and pressed it to Levin's lips.

"You don't have to do that." Levin was too surprised to say

anything else. Too surprised, and for a man his age, too con-fused. "Sit back. Take a deep breath," he finally said.

She looked better now. Her poured-out words were like vomiting; rid of them, she was weaker but at rest. She was not what he had thought. She was much shakier, more unstable. The right sort of push and she came apart. He wondered if she was half-mad, a little crazy. Maybe his information was wrong and she had been hospitalized for mental reasons. She appeared to be modish, sophisticated, independent. But she was needy, vulnerable, adrift. Hence Kaye and Weiss and now himself. Day by day, she didn't know what she was doing here. Her mud mask, down at the Dead Sea, seemed more than coincidental. Dark, wildly smeared, it was more her true face. Yet who was she? How could she exist? Was she a danger to herself? What if he wasn't here?

What an absurd and fateful situation for the two of them. Terrorism and madness. Burgers and a kiss.

17

S he was at his mercy. That was the poignant truth of the matter, bluntly put. His desires had every chance of being satisfied. If anything, his desires flamed up, as if her vulnerability was one more incitement to wanting her. She was a woman on her knees and Levin only had to be there to be the man of the hour, who was present, to supply the push.

What did that say about him, that knowing the case for mercy, he chose desire? Not much. Not to be too tough on himself, what did it say about sex?

Sex wasn't kindly. Sex was violent, like birth—the birth of a baby or a star. The sex act was literally an invasion. A welcome invasion, at its well-oiled best, but a driving act of force nonetheless. Some female thinkers went further and described all sex, the finest, as rape. They could have a point. Rape by consent. That seemed to make no sense, at first glance. But looking closer. . .

Besides: he possibly loved her. No, he could put it more strongly than that. He felt affection for her, cared about her, respected her, all the ingredients of love—just add them up.

She was his equal, little doubt about it, personally, intellectually—socially, to go the cycle. Sleeping with her wouldn't be like a master sleeping with a slave.

On the contrary, she had an edge: it wouldn't mean that much to her, the way it would to him. She herself had told him. Presumably, it meant she was a free-thinking woman, making a mature choice. But on the other hand, unfortunately, it could mean the opposite, that she had an insight into her failings and weaknesses, a sense of her shallowness, even a sense of sexual shame. How could Levin know? It wasn't a simple matter, possibly loving Deborah Kaye.

She had found a way to hang on, going back to school, teaching her Western law course. That showed strength—courage. So did her turning on Kaye, after twelve coupled years. Accusing Kaye of the murder of Weiss might be a part of that turning, that wifely twisting and turning. Whatever Kaye had killed in her, and much could be assumed, it was an understandable if bizarre leap to believe that Kaye had murdered Weiss.

If she was on the verge of leaving Kaye, it was a perilous moment. Kaye was a dangerous man. He was still her husband and not in a mood to be left. With his obsession for her, and that hyperactive brain, he could make a lot of mischief in such a tiny country. One way or another—as lovers—they would have to flee from him.

Levin imagined the two of them in Paris. There was no place finer. They would walk the Grand Boulevards, dine like the natives, breathe in the free, the carefree air. Wherever they went, they would be mistaken for father and daughter. So be it, though he would have to clear that up when they shared a bed in a hotel, because even French hotel clerks couldn't shut both eyes.

France. Birthplace of the Enlightenment. Home of Voltaire, who said that religion exists to keep the servants from stealing the silver. To keep the masters from having all the silver, in all justice he could have added that. But in the main, on the subject of faith, Voltaire was right.

Levin could see himself living in France. What he couldn't assimilate was the thought that he was French himself, at least halfway, by way of his father. There, the Holocaust had swallowed a Frenchman and spit out a Jew. Harsh words, but true. The Nazis had mass-made Jews as well as murdering them.

Here was Levin, produced in the Holy Land, but a bad fit—tied to Jerusalem, a city living on faith, feeding on faith, choking on it.

He wasn't so far removed from Deborah Kaye. There were echoes. His gradual disconnect over the years, her feverish discontent. His breakup with Miriam and her flight from Kaye. Their lies, the self-serving lies they told one another. Even the difference in their ages, a plus for both of them.

Levin no longer needed to pretend that he was on a mission for her, on a futile quest for Weiss's killer. He could be open about himself. But she seemed so fragile and unpredictable, and he would do anything to keep her trust. He still wasn't ready to tell Deborah Kaye, "I know who you are."

Sunrise over Jerusalem.

All pastel and white—cradle colors. Faded yellow stone, soiled white walls. Cradle colors dirtied by time. The rounded hills, mossy with human life, but spiky, all at odds, if you came close enough. Jutting temples, churches, mosques, and their battling prayers. The morning sun on the Dome of the Rock, gold on gold, Allah and man, begging the question of what reflected what. The Western Wall, Jewry's holiest site, a tearful, sorry remnant of itself. And the Via Dolorosa, the staggered Stations of the Cross, a challenge from its start, the most famous walking tour on earth.

All of this—and much more—could not be seen from Levin's bedroom window.

It was a decent enough apartment. The rooms were furnished with taste. The bedroom had tall cypress shutters. Shut, they promised a spectacular view. Opened, they showed a blind alley of a cobblestone street, winding and climbing, but not very far. But if he closed his eyes, Levin could smell Jerusalem, all of it, subtly fragrant, fraught with something coming, despite the heavy odds and its age.

He always had breakfast sitting at his window, breakfast being a sweet roll and special coffee, brewed by himself, his only culinary art. He drank it from a huge white cup with matching saucer, whose simple beauty never failed to please him. Two big ritual cupfuls, rich and black, sitting in his pajamas, at his open window. Levin prized this hour, too early for the mail to come, or the phone to ring, too early for either hope or disappointment.

But this morning, there was a rapping at Levin's door.

It was a surprise to hear it, and unwelcome. It was doubly irritating because there was a doorbell out there, in plain view. He hated when people knocked. They identified themselves as idiots even before he saw them.

He put down his cup and waited for them to go away. But the rapping kept on, soft . . . soft and persistent. There was something coaxing, demure about it, and Levin thought: Could it be a woman's knock? Could it be Deborah Kaye?

He hadn't shaved, hadn't brushed his teeth. His hair was a grisly tangle. But all that was thrown aside as he made a rush for the door.

"Ah, Mr. Levin," said a chubby little fellow.

Levin felt deceived—bitterly. "Next time knock like a man," he said in his growliest voice and pushed the door in the fellow's face.

But the little man stopped the door with a surprisingly firm hand. "Mr. Levin, I'm here on urgent business. You'll really want to see me."

"How urgent is urgent? Like life and death?"

"Exactly so. I have very valuable information for you. Very select."

"Who are you? Is this about Karl Weiss?"

"Please. Not out here. I promise I will inform you of every detail."

Levin stepped aside and let him in. He wore a shabby suit

and tie and carried a fat manila envelope. He had to be let in, his story heard, even if he was chubby and small and prissy, a type that made Levin very uneasy, tapping softly at his door at sunrise.

"You can call me Avram," he said when they were seated in Levin's living room, in easy chairs, face to face. "But I'm not important. I'm here to tell you that your life is in danger."

"Who sent you? How did you get my name?"

"I'm afraid that's confidential. And that's something you should welcome, Mr. Levin. You're a lucky man. There is help out there that you don't even know about—good, reliable help. Let me ask you, do you consider yourself well protected?"

"I would say so."

"Do you own a gun?"

"Yes, I have a gun."

"You see? You appreciate how risky life is these days. I'm not speaking in the abstract. I don't have to remind you that you live in Jerusalem, one of the riskiest places on the planet. And then think about your children. You have two beautiful children, am I right?"

"What do my children have to do with it?"

"Everything. Everything . . . in the long run. Need I also remind you that you are a former official of the security service. You did heroic work for them. In certain circles, that puts you at much greater risk than ordinary men. You see, Mr. Levin, I have done my homework."

"What does any of this have to do with Karl Weiss?"

"Should I recognize that name? Who is Karl Weiss?"

Levin got up. He wasn't tall, especially in slippers, but in his anger he felt like a giant hovering over the startled little man. "All right. You know all about me. What's the payoff? What's the game?"

"No game—no game. My card."

Levin grabbed it from a trembling hand.

"You're selling life insurance?"

"No. More than that. A plan plus protection. We are the only company including coverage for terrorism at a slightly higher charge. Act now and our rates are amazingly low. And we can go lower. Please . . . It's my job to sell it to people. I mean no harm."

Levin ripped the card in two. He then seized Avram by the knot of his necktie and lifted him up from the chair. Enraged, with Avram's eyes popping with fright, Levin didn't know what to do with him. He threw him back into the chair, only to immediately lift him up again and fling him toward the door. Avram fell down, saw Levin over him and crawled for the door, dragging his fat envelope with him.

"Don't hit me. Please don't hurt me. The office, they gave me your name. I came here in all good faith."

And Levin kicked him—not that viciously, and with a slipper, not a boot, but knowing that he kicked a frightened, crawling man. Kicked him for knocking at the door and not being Deborah Kaye. That was his worst, his gravest sin. And that was how Avram exited, on his hands and knees, Levin opening the door for him and slamming it after him.

Naturally, he felt rotten when he calmed down. It wasn't his practice to kick a man, humiliate a flabby little weakling. An insurance salesman—selling door to door—what a way to make a living. It seemed humiliating to begin with. Levin picked up the halves of Avram's card and held them together. Beyond repair. Life was a tough sell, all the way around.

But later in the day, Levin couldn't help but see the comical side of it. After all, it was pretty funny, somebody selling life insurance, with a small extra charge for terrorism, in Jerusalem.

18

Suppose the truth popped out by accident? Suppose he was at the university, outside the classroom where she was teaching, happened to be there when she came out? Her teaching, her identity, even her marriage, could all come out. All by accident.

Levin knew he was going to do it. He immediately wrote down the reasons for and against. He was a methodical man. That is, he could trust that his reasoning would generally support his instincts.

Reasons for: He wouldn't have to explain anything. Caught leaving the classroom, she would have to do the explaining. She would instantly feel that. But she could explain as much or as little as she wanted. He wouldn't pressure her.

Against: The deceit. An ugly negative, no way to begin a love affair. Plus, she might see through it and guess his motive. That could be fatal. Caught while stalking. It would frighten her, and no amount of blustering would help. He would have to confess the truth, plead his feeling for her, his caring. Actually, that might not be so bad. But it made little difference, one way or the other, since he was going to do it.

A phone call to the law school gave him her schedule and her classroom. That was all Levin needed. He took his camera, slinging it around his neck by a strap, a touristy look he despised, but which gave him credibility, a purpose for being there. He could be taking pictures of the campus, his old alma mater, bringing his photo album up to date. Why, hello there, Deborah. What a surprise!

It was a cool day for Jerusalem. That made it easier to be outdoors, as there was little shade on the rolling campus. Levin stood apart from the crowd passing the law school building, alone out there, as exposed as a sun dial under the blue Mount Scopus sky. He had his camera in his hands, poised to snap, but not raised enough to hide his face.

She came out on time. A couple of students were with her, earnestly talking to her. Levin took a step closer. He waved his hand. When she looked and recognized him, she was surprised but not shocked, he thought. She started toward him. But now another look crossed her face, a second sign of recognition. She came past Levin and whispered: "He's here—my husband. Go quickly. I'll meet you at the cafe."

Kaye. Kaye was here too. He had come over from the other campus. It was one recognition too many. Suppose she had greeted Levin? How to explain that to Kaye? Suppose Kaye had greeted him? How to explain that to her? Levin walked rapidly to a doorway and only then turned, hunched and hidden. Husband and wife were having a conversation. Whether it was friendly or otherwise, Levin couldn't know. At the end of it, though, Kaye kissed her. Then they parted ways, until each was out of sight.

The kiss was painful. But Levin looked at the bright side. Absent Kaye, she might have turned suspicious seeing Levin outside her classroom. She might have started wondering. But then along comes Kaye and it alters everything. Two men wouldn't be following her at the same time, two men wouldn't be out here stalking her. I'm off the hook. I'm innocent, thought Levin.

She looked out of breath when she sat down beside him in the rear of the crowded cafe. She gave the impression of hurrying to him, if not running.

"He follows me everywhere," said Deborah Kaye. "I can't get away from him. He has to teach a class now. He won't follow me here."

"And he's your husband?"

"Professor Kaye. The mathematician, the man I told you about. The man who could have murdered Karl. Yes. He's my husband."

"I saw him kiss you."

"You were watching?"

"You sounded afraid. I thought you were in danger."

"Yes. You're right. He can do that to me. I let him kiss me."

They ordered coffee because a waiter came. Neither of them looked at the other until he brought the coffee and was gone.

"I may have lied to you," she said. "I honestly don't remember. Did I tell you I was married? That I teach at the law school? It's such a relief, finally telling you everything."

He didn't think he needed to discuss her honesty. He reached and squeezed her hand, hoping she would crumble and kiss him again.

"My husband wields a lot of power in this country. Small pond—great big frog. He's a professor but he has influence everywhere, the government, industry, the army. Partly it's his family money, partly it's him, his fantastic drive, to put it kindly. He has other pet projects too. He had an arrangement with my cousin Karl. They were in a sort of art business together."

Levin felt a stab. Just when she seemed most honest she was lying again, lying about Weiss, still calling him her cousin.

"Did your husband know that you were spending time with your cousin?"

"Of course. What was there to know? Karl was family and I had no one else. Karl was a rock to me. He was good, kind, understanding. He was someone I could trust. Are you married?"

Was she changing the subject? Or actually not? "I was," Levin said. "I'm not now."

"What was she like?"

How many conversations the world over, on land, on sea, in the air, in bed, moved toward that question: your ex-husband, your ex-wife—what were they like? Of course the real question always was: Me—am I not better?

"She was nothing like you," Levin said. "And I'm nothing like Kaye."

Well said. They were both of them available for love, both escaping their old mates. The trouble was, Levin wasn't jealous of Kaye. He was trying to wipe out the memory of Weiss.

He approached it from an angle. "Karl's business with your husband. Since it involved your husband, it could have had a shadowy side, let's say, that somehow led to Karl's murder. It could give us a clue. I'd like to hear about it."

"Oh—I don't know much."

Right off, she was lying. Levin sensed that. It could only mean that she was hiding something. But then she suddenly changed direction and started talking.

"I'll tell you what I know. It had something to do with art. That's how Karl came into it, being an art historian. They bought and sold art objects—antiques. No, that's not the right word. Antiquities. Ancient pottery, urns, that sort of thing. Karl did the art side. He would go to Arabs in Jaffa, East Jerusalem, even Jordan, and buy things up. He knew what was valuable and where the sellers were. It wasn't technically legal, but they did it more for amusement than profit. Karl brought back the antiquities and my husband handled the money side."

"Being a mathematician. Good with numbers."

"Exactly."

He didn't know what to say. He was hearing his own story, a fabrication, thrown back at him, that Weiss may have been involved in the risky antiquities trade. He had made it up to justify staying on Weiss's case and seeing her again. Now she was repeating it without remembering or caring where it came from.

"God, how I wish this would all end. I'm getting so absolutely sick of everything," she said.

Levin felt warned. He stopped probing her and sat back in his chair. "Can we just sit and talk, we two?"

"I don't want to talk anymore."

"We could leave. Go somewhere else."

"Where?"

"My place."

My place. It was the fraternal twin of "What was your ex like?" Either one could follow the other. They were parts of the same evolving outcome.

"Let's go," she said.

Levin paid the bill, hailed a cab, took her up the silent stairs, unlocked his door—did all of this like a man of experience but simultaneously like a mere boy. She had never looked so desirable. He would never be able to get enough of her. Before he had any of her at all, he had this bittersweet regret.

Not much was said. She took her earrings off. Until then, he hadn't noticed her small pearl earrings. She tilted her head, catching each in her hand, a gesture so enthralling it was more like an end than a beginning. Unhurriedly, she unclothed. He itched to help but he was smart enough to let her get ready in her own sweet way. Levin undressed too. Normally he sat down to pull off his shoes and pants, but this caution seemed unwise. It would reveal more of him than he wanted. There was an abyss of over twenty years between them, never to be forgotten. He stripped the way guys did in the movies, standing up, and pretty quickly, but feeling steady on his feet as he followed her absolutely mesmerizing hips into the bedroom.

No, she wasn't like Miriam. Miriam was warmer—and more talkative, especially over the years. Talk had accompanied everything, and not always relevant talk. With Deborah Kaye, all was silent. No words, no sounds, beyond the automatic gasps. Was she enjoying herself? He worried about it. She made love effortlessly, she freely consented, but to whom? He had daydreamed more yielding in her—more force by him. He had been right about one thing: he didn't get enough of her. It was probably true that nothing equaled her taking off her earrings.

But it was their first time. It would get better, it would. Not only the lame and halt needed hope.

"Did I disappoint you?" Levin asked her, very sure that he had.

"I didn't think about it. Do you want me to?"

He laughed. "No. Forgive me. I was just acting my age."

"My husband isn't a lot younger than you."

"Have you always liked older men?" he asked.

"I don't dislike them, if I get what you mean."

"What about younger men? Younger than yourself?"

"Now you're sounding like my husband. The next thing I know, you'll be following me around too. There are no limits to my loving husband's jealousy. He's not happy if he isn't jealous."

"I'm surprised he wasn't jealous of your cousin Karl."

"Oh he was. He had no cause to be, but he was. It was extremely awkward, especially when they went into business together. Karl wanted to straighten it out. He was going to do it that day in Jaffa, after one of his antiquities trips. That's why he asked my husband to meet him there."

"Karl asked your husband to meet him that day?"

Deborah Kaye turned vague. "Did I say that? I can't remember, it could have been the other way around, my husband asking Karl to meet him. I think it must have been. What difference does it make?"

What difference? Night and day. If Weiss asked for the meeting, it reversed everything. Then Kaye could have been the one who was lured there, the original victim-to-be. Things had not turned out that way. Somehow Kaye had taken control. Kaye had told the truth when he said he blasted Weiss, but only because the plan had gone wrong, the plan hatched by Weiss and his conspiring lover, Deborah Kaye.

Levin had started the day speculating about the truth popping out by accident. What if it just had—the final truth? It would also tell him the truth about the woman who was lying beside him. What had really happened on the road to Jaffa?

"I should go now," she said with a chilling calm, suddenly sitting up. "It's always better if I'm there when he comes home."

19

A beautiful lie . . . was that Deborah Kaye?

Was that the reality Levin had been too blind to see? His good sense told him it was, that she was not to be trusted, whether or not she had conspired to murder her husband.

She was a maze of contrasts, like a puzzle of a face, a cracked mirror wherein her features, staring back, didn't meet and fit.

She was self-confident and poised—and yet erratic and unstable. Smart, a lawyer, an independent woman, who at the same time was emotionally adrift. But was this all her fault? If she was a lie, was she totally to blame?

See her tawny skin, her lips and eyes, her unaltered Hebraic face. Observe her style, her manner, her mind. So Western. So European. But now, in surviving, she was back in Asia—a refugee in the land of her fathers. Did she know who she was, did she ponder it, this woman who first appeared to him wearing a muddy Dead Sea mask?

The lie that Weiss was her cousin. Why? To cover up their intimacy? Or were there less conscious reasons? To seal their intimacy, to give it depth, foreshadowing, the taste of destiny? That they were lovers, Levin never doubted. He had seen them approach, come close, vanish together, behind the walls of the Armenian's back room.

The doubleness of Weiss himself, the youthful, puffy art historian. She called him good, strong, her rock. Levin saw him differently: callow yet crude, bookish but harsh and rough. Levin remembered the man at the bazaar in the colonial white suit, plunging forward on his walking stick, swinging it savagely at a pile of dishes, while his so innocent paramour, Deborah Kaye, melted away.

None of the above was certain. Nothing about Weiss's death was provable. Quite possibly, as she would have Levin believe, Kaye had planned it as a crime of passion from the start, Kaye the maniacal, obsessed husband.

Or, equally possible, there was no passion in it at all, except as terrorism had its roots in passion. It was a political act. Karl Weiss had been killed because he was a Jew caught driving on a lonely desert road. He was simply the victim of another random Arab attack.

But why Weiss died was almost beside the point. Deborah Kaye had become Levin's reason for staying in Jerusalem. And she filled that space whether she was a lie or not. Before her advent, he had been treading time, growing old, just staying afloat, like his fish. Deborah Kaye was his great justification. What else held him here? The Jews versus the Arabs? The museums?

True, there was his mother. She lived behind gates and locks and she would miss his visits terribly. But with her tidy life, her radio, her self-absorption, perhaps she would not. Parents were as human as children—you could overstate their love. Then there was his father, keeping him here in a different way. Levin knew he should go and see his father, that it had been months since his last visit, if you could visit a nightshirt and slippers, with a headstone of a face to remind you who he was. How much did he owe his father? Did he owe him the future direction of his life? He would certainly visit him soon. But like so many other times, he couldn't make himself go yet.

He went to the movies, which got him out of the present tense and into a distant world. He was lucky. An art cinema was showing an old film noir with both Bogart and Cagney, perhaps the only film they made together, in old studio black-and-white, so luridly lit you could smell the celluloid. Bogart and Cagney—up there on the screen like two titans before everything split, never to come together again. It felt very strange, coming back into the daylight, into Jerusalem's up-to-the-minute black-and-white suspense.

He thought incessantly about her. If she was a lie, a romantic delusion, he would know it soon enough. She would unravel. Blemishes, a kind of moral squalor would appear. She would no longer seem beautiful. In the beginning, he hadn't thought her so beautiful. She had become beautiful over time, because of his feelings about her. That same process would undo itself if she proved false. Disillusionment—it struck all the time, with couples, jobs, beliefs, everything. Did Levin believe any of this claptrap? Yes and no. He was a cynic. Once, peace of mind lay in having no hope. But here he was, on the verge of extinction, and she was amour, passion, life.

Surprisingly, they had no plan to meet again. In the flush of love-making, he had simply not looked into the future. She, who planned all her moves, a given for a double life, had not mentioned anything either. Levin had to hope she would phone him. He couldn't appear at the university again. Too aggressive—too much like Kaye. Besides, Kaye might also be there again, with disastrous results this time. Did he dare pick up the phone himself, call her at home, now that she admitted who she was?

Levin sat at his telephone, his fingers touching it, befriending it. To make calling easier, he imagined his opening sentence to her:

"Hello, it's me. I've been thinking a lot about you."

"Me too," he would hear her say. "I've been thinking about you."

It was just like his adolescent days. Back then, he would

hang up scared if the father answered the phone. Now, he would hang up if the husband answered. Same old Levin, same nervous, pudgy hand around the phone. But the stakes were different now. The husband was a jealous madman. He would jump at the meaning of a hung-up call. Levin didn't want to ignite Kaye, not if he could help it. So several times he got up from the chair, walked around the room, before coming back to sit with the phone.

It rang. It rang twice—he was just too surprised by the first ring. But when Levin picked up the phone, it wasn't the caller he expected it to be.

It was Kaye.

"I want to see you. Don't tell me no. I'm at the university, in my office."

"What's this about?"

"I think you can guess. And Levin, do make it fast. I'm waiting for you, my friend."

Levin took a taxi. He wouldn't make Kaye wait. He brought along his pistol, wearing a jacket to hide the shoulder holster. What did Kaye want? His tone went beyond urgent. It sounded ominous. "My friend," as uttered by Kaye, could mean friend or the acid opposite.

It was after dark, their old consulting hour. Across this side of the campus, the paths and buildings seemed silenced for the night. The math department secretary was long gone. Kaye was alone in his office—primed and ready—the moment Levin appeared.

"Now she's fucking somebody else."

"Your wife?"

"My wife. Of course my wife." Kaye's lips smiled in disgust. "At it again. How long is Veiss dead? A few weeks? Her cunt isn't dry yet. But she goes out and finds someone else."

"Amazing."

The worst thing had not happened. Kaye wasn't pointing a

finger at him. Levin sat down beside the desk. "How can you be so sure?"

"I'm sure. I wish I weren't. But then, I'd have to be an idiot. Instead I'm too brilliant for my own good. Not many people would understand that. I am too brilliant for my own good."

Levin thought he understood it. He even felt a twinge of sympathy for Kaye and his superactive brain.

"She invites suspicion. She really does. Maybe she doesn't care. She always seems somewhere else. I mean, when I come home she's there, but only superficially. In transit. In silhouette. She won't answer my questions, and I'm not bashful about asking them. Tonight, I went through her dirty underwear. I'm not congratulating myself. I had access so I did it. I knew I'd find scum and I was right. Whose scum? Whose handsome prick? I thank God that I'm not easily humiliated. All I felt was hate. Pure, purifying hate. I wanted to strangle the both of them."

Levin asked as blankly as he could: "So what do you want with me?"

"I want this man. The fucker's name, his resume, all of it. I want you to follow her again."

Kaye opened a drawer and flung a pair of panties on the desk.

"And I want this genetically analyzed. It may lead us nowhere, but at least it's a beginning."

"I can't do that," said Levin.

"You have your contacts at Security. They have laboratories. You can have it done."

"No," said Levin. "I cannot do that."

Kaye stared at him. "So be it," he said at last and threw the panties back into the drawer. "I won't push it. You know your own business. I'll find someone else to do the panties. You just follow her, the way you did before."

Or what? You'll find someone else to do it? Is that the fix

I'm in? Breathing deeply, Levin could feel his pistol against his chest. He wasn't planning on using it. But Kaye was uncanny. A wrong word, an ambiguous answer, and he might leap to a conclusion both wild and brilliant. To carry through, he might very well have a gun of his own in his drawer. As for following her, Levin didn't doubt that he would find someone else for the job, an authentic, proficient private eye. And that would probably be the end of everything between himself and Deborah Kaye. As absurd as it was, he would have to agree to follow her. He would figure out what the hell that might mean when he got out of here.

"I'll be glad to do it," said Levin. "I don't see a problem. I'll start on it tomorrow."

"Thanks, friend."

Now that the talk was over, Kaye seemed to sag with relief. Far from menacing, he looked plaintive and weak and exhausted.

"I don't trust her," he said. "But I love her more than I hate her. That's the dilemma."

20

He wasn't in such a fix—once Levin put his mind to work:

Stay friends with Kaye. Pretend to follow her. Keep a bogus account of it. Faithfully report this account to Kaye. Meanwhile, meet and be with her.

Levin took his pistol with him always now. Carrying it, he felt confident, complete. He was rather like a matron who had discovered just the right ensemble for herself, the one most flattering. Broadbrimmed Panama hat, slightly tight jacket, loaded gun and holster under the jacket. In the mirror, he looked and felt interesting, well worth knowing. He was eager to see himself out on the street.

He added his camera to the outfit. This time he actually used it. Going to a fashionable concourse, he spotted a handsome, expensively tailored man, not young, with bold features, a power-broker type. Levin walked behind the man, snapping pictures of his back. When the man stopped to look in a store window, Levin stood to the side and sneaked a striking profile shot. He took pictures of other men in various locations that day. There was a big athletic man in running shorts, and a longhaired, sensitive poetic type, and a sleek-haired punk with a baby face. There were others, a good male cross section. He had the photos developed in an hour and sat at home evaluating them.

They were her possible lovers. Levin would choose the finalist, the man caught on camera, who suspiciously appeared wherever she did. Levin would choose and Kaye, looking at the pictures, would fill in the maddening details for himself. The power type, for example, would intimidate with his boldness, his worldly look, his seasoned handsomeness. The scruffy punk would suggest a completely different story, cheap, dirty, degrading. They and all the other would-be lovers would be credible to Kaye. Indeed, all were credible to Levin, which was not something he wanted to think about.

Which to choose? How best to worry and misdirect Kaye? Levin was in no rush to decide. A week of pretending to shadow her should go by before he reported to Kaye.

But meeting with Deborah—that couldn't wait. Levin sent a note to her at the law school, where it would sidestep Kaye, who undoubtedly opened her mail at home. His note flew off:

Must see you. When and where?

Our museum? The Armenian's?

The cafe? All yours, L.

Her answer came back, curt, vague, unsigned:

Not now. Sorry. Try me again.

He almost ripped the note up. Her breeziness stunned him. She simply killed his appetite for her, for a while. But as he knew it would, his appetite came back. It was a very starved appetite. He saw good reasons for such a note. She could be afraid to make a move right now. She could be not entirely trusting. Why should she be? And hadn't she asked him to try her again?

He did. He sent her a second note, identical to the first. It was a trick he borrowed from international diplomacy, where you repeat your original offer as if it had never been received, and hope that something has changed at the other end. His diplomacy paid off. She would meet him, she wrote Levin, at the museum. She named the day and time.

The Tower of David Museum. He reentered as if it were a starting point, from which they would slip off to somewhere else to be alone. So the stony cragginess didn't worry him, or the roofless openness, or the guided tours passing through. There were two tour groups, Germans and Japanese. How tame they looked today, those demons of the past from World War Two. Was there an important lesson here? Would Jews and Arabs cease being enemies someday, as if a harsh word had never been exchanged? Could human hearts and minds actually be changed? Would Deborah Kaye meet Levin here today?

Levin knew that she would not. He waited another half-hour, small change, considering his total investment. But even then, he couldn't resign himself to the hopeless truth. For no good reason whatever, none, except his gnawing emptiness, he took a taxi to their last meeting place, the cafe.

Their table in the back was occupied. He took the closest one nearby, and sat down, with his utterly false sense of belonging. As before, the place was noisy with young people, high school and college age.

Very quickly, before a waiter came, a young girl popped down beside him. Levin looked around. There were still some unoccupied tables.

"Hello, Daddy," she said.

Levin's eyes took her in. She had big sunglasses. A striped T-shirt rippled over her girlish breasts. Her washed-out blue-jeans hugged her tight. Was she all of seventeen?

Levin said uncomfortably: "I'm sorry. But I'm waiting for someone."

"Okay if I wait with you?"

He shrugged. It wasn't much of an answer. But he didn't know what to say. A couple of minutes passed. The girl didn't stop looking at him, assuming there were open eyes behind those big dark glasses.

"Are you all right? Can I get something for you?" Levin said.

"Sure. I wouldn't mind a chicken sandwich. Maybe we could split it. Half for me and half for you."

The waiter came. Levin ordered the sandwich, and a cup of coffee for himself. She said to him, looking solemn:

"I'm real hungry, Daddy."

Could this be literally true? Was she a teenage runaway, out begging for something to eat? Levin felt her hand brush his thigh. Perhaps she was only spreading out her napkin. She had moved very close to him. She could be older than she looks, he thought. It was impossible to tell these days. She could even be a prostitute. Why? Was he so far gone, so ogrish, that he would have to pay for sex? There were all those stories about young girls, admittedly all mixed up, who yearned for father figures.

He wondered if her girlfriends were watching, if she had plopped down to tease him—if that was their little game. Levin wondered, but he didn't look around, because he didn't want to know.

She reached out her hand and pulled his hat brim down a bit, slouching it over one eye.

"That's better. That's how you should look. I love that. I could go for you in a really big way."

She should feel the hard gun under his jacket, he thought. That would interest her, wouldn't it, if she thrilled to the slouch of his hat. So what if her girlfriends were watching? Let them watch. It seemed a fair exchange, she teasing him, he letting her—enjoying her—not so much as a real girl as a paper one, a cut-out, the international teen, with her brazen clinging T-shirt and her jeans.

It was enjoyable. But he got up when their order came, putting money on the table, more than enough.

"I'm sorry," said Levin. "But I'm running late."

She picked up her half of the sandwich.

"Bye, Daddy. I'll never forget you."

Levin didn't push on to the Armenian's, that other past meeting place. Deborah Kaye wouldn't be found there either. He went home. Of course she had once been there too, most definitely there. So he was following her after all, as he had promised Kaye he would do, except that he was following a phantom. He reflected on Kaye, how their situations were completely different, yet becoming more the same. Neither of them possessed her. Neither understood her. Kaye had referred to her as a silhouette. She was a bit like the teenager in sunglasses and bluejeans, baffling and mysterious to men. Did that mean that she hadn't grown up? Or that they, the men, hadn't sufficiently grown?

He would have to report to Kaye soon. What to report? The absurdity of the matter aside, he deeply resented Kaye, the one who had pulled him into all this, the obsessed mathematician, the betrayed husband who at least saw her every day and perhaps still had sex with her, women and men being what they were.

Make Kaye pay for all that. It might be petty, and it wouldn't bring her any closer, but Levin would feel better if Kaye suffered more. The pain would be distributed more evenly. Justice would be served.

Levin sorted through his photographs of the men and mailed his final selection to Kaye. It came down to two strong contenders, and Levin couldn't bear to choose. So he passed along the both of them—the rich and handsome power-broker, and the scruffy baby-faced punk. He attached a note:

She's too clever to be photographed
with anyone. But I'm right on her
tail and I think I'm getting close.
Do you recognize either of these men?
Or—I hate to say this—both?

21

His mother turned her radio up louder. If he was here, she always did this when a bloody bulletin broke in. When she was alone, it would be different. He knew she shrank with thoughts of Leningrad and switched it off. But with him here, she let it blare, scream. It did her good, apparently, to hear her own life's nightmare reaching everyone in a general alarm.

"Listen," she told him, "listen," as if Levin had a choice, raising her finger at the little radio on the kitchen counter, a home appliance gone berserk between the toaster and the coffee pot.

The bulletin announced another terrorist attack, this time a suicide bomber who had detonated himself in a crowded marketplace. The calm and booming voice gave the details: the location, the method, the damage, the number of dead and injured as this became known. The arrival of police and ambulances was reported, along with the presence of government officials. The bulletin had another important aspect. Listeners could guess if anyone they knew might be at the scene. Phone calls could then be made. People could rush to the location, and stand as close as they could get.

Today the bomb attack was not far off. He and his mother heard the sirens on the radio as they were hearing them shrieking through the streets. Levin went to the window, not that he could see anything from here, but it was impossible not to look from a window. No one they knew was in apparent danger, his father in the nursing home, his children abroad, his old associates not likely to be in a poorish marketplace in the Old City. He could assume that Deborah Kaye wasn't there either, not being her kind of ambiance. The dread he felt wasn't for anyone in particular. Call it animal. Call it tribal. He was a Jew to his core at these moments. Terror accomplished what religious conviction could never do. Automatically, like it or not, you were kin to people you liked and admired and people you mistrusted and despised, each and every one of them. Emotionally, a barbed wire fence was thrown around you, keeping the threat out, the particular threat of the moment. But the same wire fenced you in. That was the unmentioned thing about terror. The outside threat wasn't all you shrank from. The kinship threatened you too. The closeness could also make you want to pack your bags and leave.

"You're going?" his mother asked, for Levin had put his cup and saucer in the sink and was coming to kiss her goodbye. "Why are you going now? Where?"

"I can stay . . . They're almost winding this up."

She pushed him away. "No—go. Go. You've already made up your mind, so go. My God. Where did you get that hat?"

The streets were very quiet, the usual aftermath, converging sirens and traffic all gone. Black smoke rose above the Old City skyline, a guide to the market place. Levin walked to the scene. The dead and seriously injured had been taken away. Police moved within a barricaded area, among the shattered stalls, their splattered goods. It was a Hassidic neighborhood and they made up most of the lingering crowd. A few looked dazed. But as victims of the situation they always sprang back to life fast. You had to admire them for that. Other Jews carried on, went heavily about their business. The Hassidics, whose business was God on earth, were soon darting about with their black coats and doll's curls, their drabness and joy. Peculiar people. But of course Levin was the curiosity here,

not them. Off by himself, he could have been a man from anywhere in the world. Their occasional glances at him weren't
unfriendly. They might have welcomed his sympathy. But
Levin steered clear of them. They made him uncomfortable.
They made him feel like a stranger in this country, they who
were so much at home here.

Could he really be staying in Jerusalem because of
Deborah Kaye, another man's wife, a woman from another
generation, whom he could hardly be said to know? Perhaps
he knew her as well as he ever would. They would meet by
prearrangement. Their conversation would touch on this or
that subject. She would take her earrings off the same way
every time. Go to bed with him, get up, get dressed, go home.
There could be more, a growing attachment, who could say?
He didn't know if she would leave Kaye, or if he would ask
her to. So would he die for her, as Karl Weiss may have done?
Kill for her, hypothetically the case with Kaye? He might do
both, but killing, dying, Levin couldn't believe that it would
ever come close to that.

Kaye called—just about on schedule.

"I'm looking at these photographs. I could puke. Who are
these guys?"

"Don't jump to conclusions," Levin said. "They're men I
thought worth photographing, just following my instinct. We
don't have any proof of anything yet."

"Who are they? What are their names?"

"I was thinking you might know."

"How? Am I a crystal ball? I never saw either one of them,
the bastards. You're wrong if you think I'm surprised. The
smooth, sophisticated type . . . the cheap young pug. She could
take on both of them. Old and young, smooth and rough.
Different feel—different friction. No, I'm not surprised, my
friend, only hurt and saddened. I'm almost afraid to ask, what's
next? Better photographs? Names and places?"

"Slow down. I'm being very careful. We assume I'm on the trail, but I have to keep my distance. I don't want to make your wife suspicious. I also have to caution you. These are only photographs. They may not show the right man or men. They were just the likeliest I could find."

"Don't be so modest. I look at them and I think the same things you do. I'm grateful to you, Levin. You do good work. When will I hear from you again?"

"The minute I have something new, I'll call you."

"Something new. That's quite a way to put it, isn't it. My wife has something new."

Kaye hung up. Levin pictured him at his desk, staring at the photographs, his eyes going from one to the other, the power-broker and the punk, envisioning his wife's sexual reach. Did he suffer, along with his hunger to know? Or did he love to contemplate her desires? It was difficult to feel sorry for Kaye. Either he was madly obsessed, or playing a game, creating a fascinating new wife for himself, a woman of casual lust, the Deborah Kaye whom Levin was supposed to be following.

Obsession or a game, this didn't explain the facts, which included a past lover, Weiss, and a lover-in-waiting, himself. She kept metamorphosing in his mind, muddled by Kaye's version of her, the affair with Weiss, his own unsettled feelings about her. He had to see her. Make contact. He had to nail her down. That's what sex was, for a man, in a way—nailing the woman down. Screwing was nailing. She was fixed under you for a fixed moment in time. Nailed. "I love you" achieved the same end, doing it in words. "You're mine."

He climbed Mount Scopus again, to the old campus, not a heroic feat, but high enough to symbolize one, when he reached his goal, rather excited and short of breath. It was half an hour before her law class let out. Levin stationed himself in the shade of a nearby doorway. The half-hour passed. Other classes broke. Students emerged, sending him out of the doorway and into the open glare. He looked all around but today Kaye was nowhere in sight. Still, Levin pulled his hat brim down.

Crowds of people passed before him. Watching for her face was like standing in a galaxy: every other face, every other form, was cosmic waste, dark matter, counting for nothing. That was how it felt, watching for someone as he was, waiting for Deborah Kaye. But to what end; why was he here? Simply to see her? To speak to her? To snatch her away?

He saw her. He saw, in the same drawn breath, that Kaye was with her, just behind her. All this time, Kaye had been inside. More than ever, Kaye didn't trust her. He couldn't rush here and then wait for her outside her classroom anymore. He stuck to her, perhaps stood guard through her teaching, hung tight.

Levin's photographs—the sight of the two men who were enjoying his wife had made Kaye even more vigilant than before. He couldn't stay away for a moment. He couldn't let her out of his sight, not after viewing those maddening, phony photographs.

That was Levin's explanation for Kaye's being here today. Right or wrong, the reality was the same. He couldn't get near her. It was time for him to go home. But he didn't. The student crowd had moved on to other places and left him standing all alone. The galaxy was gone. And so they saw him too.

It was an exquisite moment. Everyone saw everyone— Kaye, Deborah Kaye, Levin. But no one spoke. They stood more still, if anything. It was in no one's interest to do otherwise. Deborah Kaye didn't want to recognize a pursuing lover. Kaye didn't want to recognize the man he had asked to follow her. And Levin couldn't be seen as knowing either of them.

Everyone saw everyone and nothing changed. For the three of them, it was like an eternal moment, when time stood still, nothing changed, and nothing ever would.

22

He thought once again about France.

Europe was just across the sea. The blessed Mediterranean that washed ashore here rolled up onto French beaches—prettier, sandier beaches, less gunfire too. Plane or ship could swiftly transport him there. He was the most portable of beings. He had a pension and a passport, just add another suitcase or two. Throw in the travel arrangements and he could be settled in Paris in a week. His mother could follow or not. His father wouldn't miss them.

France the country seemed wonderful. He wasn't as enthusiastic about the French. He had met enough of them, here and abroad, and wherever they were they felt superior. It was a trifle insulting, even if in some ways it was true. They certainly knew how to live, to cultivate everything they had. The world gave them credit for that. They took an ordinary piece of meat, or a plain-looking woman, or a thin idea, and they added sauce, style, cleverness, to get a beautiful result. They weren't the most profound people on earth. But maybe that was the source of their flair for life. Jews, on the other hand, might be too profound for their own good. They weren't satisfied with superficial appearances, from Jesus to Freud and Einstein. In fact, they were a basically dissatisfied people. They also felt superior, another word for chosen, but it didn't always make them happy like the French. Their Jewish superiority could make them suffer. Here they were, in their proud little nation, on the rim of Asia, hanging on stubbornly for dear life. Their own nation. Was it really worth the heartache, the terror, the death?

Escape to Europe, as his weary ancestors had done. Leave the unforgiving desert, let the unforgiving Arabs make it bloom. Or suppose the American evangelicals were right about Armageddon and the Good Lord's plan to start it here? Another sound reason for packing. This might be the promised land for some, he conceded. But Levin couldn't say that his own future held much more promise than the apocalypse. If he had been too alone before, that was all changed now. From Kaye to Deborah Kaye to Weiss and back, the tale seemed too tangled with people ever to lead anywhere.

Levin grew thoughtful, though. Suppose he was being too hasty, too dismissive of those who found a home here. Maybe the problem was not in his situation, so much, as in his view— his point of view, to some extent, but also his actual view—from his window.

Opening his back shutters to a small blind street, morning after morning, had to have a depressing effect. His world shrank to an alley before he ever went out. Plus, being so isolated here, except for his fear of meeting Miriam. He was sick of the colorless neighborhood too. Move—that was the answer. But he wouldn't have to move all the way to France. Finding another place in Jerusalem could be enough.

Another place in Jerusalem. Change addresses and change your luck. Levin was excited. Was it by accident that the first place he thought of was Karl Weiss's old digs at the edge of the Arab quarter?

He remembered a sunny view of a spacious square and the lively fringes of an Arab bazaar. It might prove liberating, in itself, to live so close to the alien other. It was a very decent room. He remembered liking the landlady too, feeling compassion for her, an abandoned mother with a small child, who badly needed a boarder's rent. They might become friendly, giving him someone to talk to, besides simplifying his laundry and breakfast. How much of a nuisance could one little child be? It was just the one room, true, but how much space did he need?

Cousin Karl's old room. Levin felt a sense of rightness about it, a seductive symmetry. As she must have done with Weiss, Deborah Kaye would come to him there. She would feel drawn, even if Weiss and his baggage were gone. Lover or close cousin, nothing needed to be explained. She would understand what Levin was conveying to her.

Levin went there, did so immediately, almost afraid he might change his mind. He was apprehensive right up to the moment he rang the bell. But he felt a rush of confidence when the same woman holding her baby opened the door.

She seemed not to remember him. It could have been his Panama hat, or that she had so many maternal burdens on her mind. No matter. Levin went directly to the point.

"I understand you had a room for rent. Is it still available?"

"Come in."

Her neat apartment seemed just the same to him, not at all bad, given his new view of it as a place where he might live. The woman herself was much calmer than last time, almost a different woman. Before she opened Weiss's door, she stood in front of it, the baby in her arms, and recited a little piece for Levin.

"Before you see this room, there are things you should know. The most important is, it's not an ordinary room. A famous artist lived here. I'd tell you his name, but he swore me to secrecy. He was famous but a very private man, a nice man. He loved this room. He'd still be living here but he was called to America all of a sudden. I don't know why. I'm only telling you this so you'll understand about the room and why I'm asking more than I would for it."

Then she opened the door and Levin saw that the room was completely unchanged. All of Weiss's things were still here—

the paintings on the walls, the art objects on the bureau, the art books on the table, the art books piled in a corner, everything still in place.

"You can tell that he was an artist," the woman said with a smile. "Almost everything he had is still here. He took a few things away. But he left all the rest. He said I should keep it for him in case he ever came back."

No one had come for Weiss's belongings. It was clear to Levin. The woman couldn't get anyone to haul them away. Stuck with his things, she had dreamed up a story to explain them, to give the room added appeal, perhaps to hide the grisly facts of her tenant's demise.

If he ever came back . . . Cousin or lover, he already had. Levin felt suffocated in here, suffocated by a dead man. The woman opened the door to the closet for him. He flinched, expecting to see Weiss's clothes hanging there—the sweaty white linen suit. But the clothes were gone, perhaps sold off. Only the walking stick was there, leaning against the back of the closet, waiting to be seized. The woman called attention to it. "He loved to take long walks. It was sad, that he was lame."

Levin didn't open the curtains to the spacious, sunny view. He knew he would never invite Deborah Kaye to sleep with him here. Why would he? There was too much to remember, too much to obliterate. Too much left of Weiss, Karl.

"He was a very famous man," the woman reminded him as they walked back through the hall."

"It's a very nice room. I'll think about it."

"Don't take too long. If you wait, it might be gone."

Levin fled the place. The woman appeared surprised. They hadn't yet talked about the rent. He didn't feel compassion for her today, for her and her baby in her arms. Far from a picture of poignancy, they were more like a front for a fraud. Human beings learned so fast. It took your breath away. To salvage herself, she dreamed up a story, pure myth, and peddled it to people who were just looking for a room. Live where a Great One lived. Leaf through His books. Breathe the same air He breathed. Walk with His walking stick.

No, it wasn't Levin's destined room. It might be someone else's answer to a prayer—someone else's promised landlady. But not his.

23

A ringing and a ringing in the middle of the night.

The dream-writer, the prodigious hack, can find a use for this. The dream in progress takes a twist. A siren wails somehow, never telling why. It's a general alarm, that ringing in the night. It could mean anything. The world is on fire. the Gestapo is at the door. The morgue is calling.

The morgue is calling. The dreamer is stirring, the ringing is more plausible. A body is lying on a slab. Or in the emergency room, on a table. Levin saw his mother, his father, his children.

But it wasn't someone phoning him. It came from further away, and yet nearer in the end. His doorbell. They were right outside, leaning on his doorbell, the idiots. Levin was fully awake now.

They wouldn't go away. He didn't believe it was legitimate. At one o'clock in the morning, it must be a mistake, drunken idiots at the wrong door. Angry, but wary, he took his pistol from the night table drawer. He got out of bed and flicked a light on, then flicked it off, thinking more clearly, preferring the dark. He moved like a shadow—a gun, pajamas, bare feet. He considered calling through the door and asking who it was, but in an absurd way this seemed unmanly. He unlocked the door and opened it an inch.

Deborah Kaye. Yes. It was she. The unlikeliest person to be here was here. Not only that. She was suddenly the likeliest, the one person on earth needing him the most. Her whole hand was still on the bell.

"Where have you been? For God's sake, let me in."

She ran past him. It wasn't a kiss. But Levin was too elated to care. And he saw how distraught she was, her hands clawed and her hair a little wild, and she jumped when she saw his gun.

"Don't come near me with that. I've had enough shit for one night."

He rushed the pistol into the bedroom and came back switching on the lights, removing shadows, making all safe, and then taking her into his arms. She was shaking. He could feel the bits and pieces. He waited for sobs, but she held back. But they must have been close to the surface. He very nearly had to peel her off.

"Come sit. I'll get you a drink."

What a terrible thing, yet what fantastic luck. He felt revitalized, a newly oiled machine. He did everything just right. Hugged her, released her, brought her whisky, sat down opposite her, didn't intrude on her, waited patiently.

"I'm so ashamed of myself," she said, "coming to you like this."

Shame was all right. Shame was crackling with intimacy.

"I didn't know where else to go. I got in my car and drove like a demon. I'm sure I wasn't followed."

"He'd follow you? In the middle of the night?"

"You don't know him. He has somebody else following me. He told me that tonight."

"That's very hard to believe. Maybe he was lying to you, just to frighten you."

"No. This man, a private detective, took pictures for him."

"Pictures of you?"

"Pictures of two men. He said they're sleeping with me, both of them. Except that sleeping was not the word he used."

"This is so ridiculous."

"That's what I told him. Then he showed the pictures to

me—two completely strange men. I swore that I had never seen them before. He threw the pictures in my face. He was vile."

"Did he hurt you?"

"No, he never hurts me. Yes—he slapped me."

Levin stood up. He paced, grim-faced and thoughtful, the oiled male machine. But inwardly, Levin squirmed, blaming and despising himself.

"You did the right thing," he told her. "It's an impossible situation. I don't see how you can go back to him."

He looked toward her, not directly. He didn't know what he wanted her to say, what he was wishing for. She didn't help him, sitting limply, with her unbrushed hair, sipping the last of her drink. She seemed very much a figure of pity, though that could change and in an instant—she might simply straighten her back. If she was alone and miserable, he was the immediate cause of it. He couldn't think seriously about going to bed with her now. That's what whores were for; whether they were in pain or not was beside the point.

There was the bigger picture. He couldn't confess the part he had played in all this, that he was Kaye's photo-snapping private detective. To confess would be the finish of everything. At some point, Kaye might blurt the truth. Levin figured he could rely on Kaye's obsessiveness here, to keep the plot boiling. Yet he didn't see how he could go on seeing and deceiving her. It was an impossible situation. He had no idea how it would end, this night or their lives.

Another ringing in the night—this time, the telephone. He wasn't sorry to escape to the bedroom for a minute, no matter who might be calling.

It was Kaye.

"She's out to wipe me off the face of the earth. She's gone."

The bedroom door was wide open. "I'm very sorry to hear that," said Levin. "I'll call you first thing in the morning."

"The icy cunt left me—walked out."

Levin lowered his voice. "I'll call you in the morning. I can't talk now."

"Oh?"

"I really can't."

"How come you can't?"

"My ex-wife is here . . . we're reconciling."

"Fucking?"

"You might say that."

"My God . . . Everybody but me."

"You're going to be all right," said Levin loudly, to cut him off. "Try and sleep. I'll talk to you in the morning."

He stayed there for another minute in case Kaye called him right back, a distinct possibility. But the phone didn't ring.

"A friend," Levin said to Deborah Kaye. "He sometimes calls me during the night. He has problems."

She smiled at him. It was a complete change of mood. "Everyone comes to you."

He wished he trusted her. It would have made everything much closer to normal. But she had a way of seeming untruthful, even shrewd, when she probably was being sincere. Was he being used? Why was she really here?

"Will you go back to him?" Levin asked.

"Will I go back? That's a fair question. Are you sure you want to know? I mean, if I said I want you, I crave you, wouldn't that be what you want to hear, not whether or not I reside with my husband? It might be a lot more convenient for you too. I don't know what to tell you, Levin. I don't think about my feelings much. That probably surprises you, since I'm a woman, crawling with feelings, right? But I really don't think about them. *C'est moi*—that's me. That's what the French say. Do you know French? My husband didn't slap me. I only said that because I'm angry. But that part is true. I'm very angry. He really showed me those pictures and he has a vile tongue. But it's still not a whip. I've been whipped and I can tell you there's a difference. Now, doesn't that fascinate you, Levin, that I've been whipped? Wouldn't you love to know the details, did I request it or not? It might tell you what kind of a girl I am. I need men, fortunately or not. I'm normal in that respect, normal to a fault, you could say. But it isn't for the sex. I put up a good front, but I'm not wild about sex. When I was about ten, one summer on a farm, I had some insect bites, worse than mosquito bites. They were all over my legs. I scratched and scratched until I was bloody and it was sheer heaven, the pleasure. I've never had sex like that. On a summer night I still long for those bugs. I'll have sex with you, Levin. You can expect that. But it won't mean what you want it to mean. It won't."

She was telling the truth, he realized—the kind of girl she was, allowing for a little exaggeration. Levin wished he were satisfied and could rest with that. But he couldn't hold back.

"What about Weiss? Was it different with Weiss?"

"I might as well go home, if you're going to discuss Karl. I don't understand why Karl should have anything to do with you. Can't you forget about Karl?"

Again, painfully, he believed her. She thought that one lover, in the flesh or gone, could exist side by side with another. In her mind, they weren't a crowd. It didn't seem female to Levin, the same as when she said that she never thought about her feelings. Would she also insist that she never looked in the mirror?

"My husband praised you," she said. "That was the first I heard about you. He pictured you as a secret agent type, a man who had used a gun, a clever man of action. He was full of compliments. But you can be sure he wouldn't have raved about you if you were young and handsome. He's too envious ever to do that. I don't know why he talked about you, but he made sure I knew you were past your prime, that you weren't the man you used to be. Maybe that was the idea, to pretend to praise another man while giving himself a boost. How old are you, Levin? Sixty, sixty-one, did he say? That was about perfect for him. But it was perfect for me too. I was lost after Karl died. I kept thinking of what my husband had told me about you. You were just what I needed. I had to get your attention and I had a lucky chance that day at the Dead Sea. I discovered I liked you. Next, I asked you to find out if my husband had murdered Karl. I thought that would give us a reason to keep meeting. But I wasn't lying to you. My husband may have murdered Karl. I'm aware of that. I think it was a terrorist, but it could have been my husband. They were enemies, and they both had reasons for it, one way or another. That's all I'm going to say about Karl. He's gone. I need you, Levin. I like you. If it makes you happier, I want you. You're an honest man. You're warm and wise and strong. You have your own needs, but you're not young. I'm being blunt. It'll be all right, I promise you. Don't ask me to see into the future, if I'm going to leave my husband or when. I can't tell you. You don't know him. He's not always what he seems to be. And I owe him a lot, dating back a long time. I've thought about you, Levin—gone back and forth, anyway, in my mind. But I need time. Hasn't a woman ever told you that? I know it's selfish of me, what I'm asking. I'm frightened in Jerusalem. I might be frightened any place I go. But I think I feel less frightened when I'm with you."

Levin wondered, should he go and put his arm around her and take her hand in his? Was this the proper moment for that? He was warm and wise and strong—good big things. But at the same time he felt diminished and hurt, to be wanted because he wasn't the man he used to be.

"I'm leaving now, Levin. Do you want to make love before I go?"

He smiled. "No. Not tonight, my dear. We'll save that small pleasure for our future." It wasn't the worst beginning for a love affair: he wanted, in the sweetest way, to hurt her too.

He smelled her perfume after she had gone. In her rush to flee her husband, not brushing her hair, she had put on fresh perfume. What did that signify about her? Not much. He didn't know that he had gained anything enduring tonight. Deborah Kaye had come to him. He had reached that point in the adventure, a sort of resting place. But as far as the rest of the way was concerned, where did that leave him?

The phone rang. Divining who it was, Levin let it ring a bit before he picked it up. Kaye's voice jumped out of it like a happy puppy out of a box.

"It's all right. It's all right! You can relax, my friend. She's back."

24

L ife goes on. Or not. Or somewhere in between. Levin lived in that pause. He had stopped dreaming about France, or a new apartment with a better view. Compared to others in Jerusalem, his life was bearable, and sometimes more.

Anxiety, the fear of terror, was shared by all. They were all hooked up to the same nervous system, the same bloodstream. News of a bomb exploding could make you feel the slush of your body parts. You didn't ride a bus if you still had half a brain. You didn't sit near a cafe window and ask for a blast of flying glass. You didn't go through the mirror into the Arab half of town. You tried to be home before dark, but the noon sun was no lucky charm either. The suicide bomber could be the man or woman standing next to you. The multireligious air was almost too dense to breathe.

There were no more museums for Levin for consolation. The doors to the past had closed for him and put a sign up: "All gone and never coming back." He simply smiled at the ghoulish evangelicals, out looking for Armageddon, and at their opposites, the Hassidic Jews, dizzy with present joy. To be honest about it, he felt closer in mood to the Christians. In a minor apocalyptic moment, he threw the last of his fish away.

He had no contact with Arabs, not his old friend Ali or the random taxi driver. He had no reason to speak to an Arab. The closest he came to them was Miriam, who was their empathetic advocate. He and she would collide on the street when Levin couldn't avoid her. Her gray braids annoyed him, her matching idealism annoyed him, as did everything else. She spoke of marches and petitions, and the Jews as the new Goliath, versus the young sling-shooting Arabs. She talked of understanding and trust, and the need for partnership in making peace. He didn't disagree with her. It wasn't only because he wanted to escape her that he didn't argue with her. But she was so predictably hopeful, so full of the same old sanity and good will, that it always left him more cynical than before. Afterward, he often wrote his children to stay where they were, and not think about coming home soon.

Deborah Kaye. Whatever meat there was in his life was provided by Deborah. Making love was meat. So was love itself, or reaching for it. So was missing her, which was most of the time. He formed the idea that missing someone and having someone were viscerally identical, that in your gut, presence and absence, full and empty, felt the same. Feeling was deaf and dumb. What spoke was the story, the events that went along with it. For him, it was a consoling idea. Deborah was with him even when she was not. He wondered if the same idea could apply to religion, faith, the existence or not of a God. Presence was absence. Loving meant missing. It was a mischievous idea, a neat way to explain how he could live in the Holy Land.

She would come to his apartment. It was never at night again. The closed shutters, the spells in bed, their falling asleep, only simulated night, as if they were a normal couple keeping normal hours. They talked more than Levin had anticipated, about her Western law course, his past intelligence work, happenings around the world. Her conversation was crisp, smart and modish, like her clothes. She had no interest in politics, didn't follow local events, was a non-believer, knew no religious Jews. So it was remarkable, given all that, how like Israel she was, as if being so thoroughly isolated in this country made her so much like this solitary country.

She assured him that Kaye wasn't having her followed. That danger had ceased, for the time being anyway. Kaye wasn't hounding Levin either, by phone or otherwise, a fact that Levin naturally kept to himself. He wondered if she kept secrets of her own. It might explain her freedom to come here, and why Kaye's mad jealousy was apparently under control. You never knew the truth about a husband and wife, the bent rules they lived by. Had she remembered ways of placating Kaye that had worked in the past, ways he didn't want to think about, he with the wide-open mind who used to allow himself to imagine everything, however forbidden? Or perhaps Kaye had merely milked all the sick pleasure he could from this obsession and had moved on to another. Professional? Political? Levin didn't need to know. It was enough that Deborah was here, though she discouraged any talk about the future. He told himself that in this they were like friends. Why would friends talk about their future? Neither of them said, "I love you." The difference in their ages made that difficult, even ludicrous. At least, this was Levin's understanding of the matter. When he felt like saying it, it still went unsaid.

He never told his mother about Deborah. As far as she, Anna, was concerned, her son was divorced, his children grown, his life as near to being completed as her own. Also, he was hers again. Now, when he visited, she expected him to stay with her longer. She had his favorite meals waiting for him, no matter the time of day. She reclaimed him with food and with memory, bringing up the distant past—his childhood, her own—mixing up her memories with his. She had never been religious, but now she celebrated the Jewish holidays, lit the Sabbath candles, rekindled family traditions, not for some Jehovah in the sky, but for him. Never mind that she never went to worship in a temple. The object of her religion was to bring him home. That made all of Judaism true. Levin understood all this about her. To have mentioned another woman would have dumbfounded her, besides the questions it would have raised. It would have frightened her, and she was frightened enough for an old woman, with her siren-screaming radio, living here and being walled up again in Leningrad. So the name of Deborah Kaye was never mentioned. She wasn't the only one. It was the same with Anna's husband—Joseph—Levin's father.

Joseph's room in the dementia ward was his alone. Space was scarce, but roommates had not worked out, not even the stillest. He could not live with anyone, commune with anyone, bear to have anyone near him. Lately, his intense resistance seemed to be lessening. If so, the staff told Levin, it was because his general condition was growing worse.

His room was at the end of a long straight corridor. Levin had to pass the open doors and the parked wheelchairs—the portrait gallery that hardly changed. The unseeing stare. The gaping jaw. The mumbled chant. The moan. Anna no longer came here at all. Levin visited infrequently, if you could call his sitting with Joseph a visit. It was more a witnessing, a duty, an easing of his conscience. He was well enough known, he and his credentials, that no one bothered him at security and he was allowed to walk to Joseph's room alone. He never hurried. It was a wasted courtesy, but when he reached Joseph's door, he always knocked.

Even normal aging is a sort of horror movie over time. Here comes the sight that has all along been dreaded, the slow turning of the moth-eaten face. It was never easy for Levin, no matter how many times he saw it. Joseph was bearded, a roughly trimmed beard, because it was impossible to shave him. He was toothless, because they were not able to refit him for his lost false teeth. For the simplest procedure, orderlies had to sneak up on him and hold him down. His fear gave the frail wreck surprising strength. He kicked and screamed. He was so terrified of them that he was almost too much for them, except in a pack, and then the pack confirmed his terror. They were guards—he was back in Auschwitz. The psychiatrists offered this as a hypothetical explanation. In a way, his fading memory had jammed. Over and over, Joseph was reliving Auschwitz.

He was awake, sitting on the edge of his bed in his green nightshirt. Levin shut the door but remained there. He knew that Joseph was frightened. Perhaps he had been tranquilized, which they had to do at times: he sat, saying nothing. But suddenly he crossed his legs. To protect himself? Who knew why? At the onset of his illness, he had vowed to Anna that before his mind was completely gone, he would shoot himself. He had not kept his vow. Now it was impossible to look at him and imagine a self to shoot. Here in the present, he knew no one. He had forgotten France. He no longer knew about Israel, about independence, triumph, sudden terror, a new and different war. If he was anywhere, he was back in Auschwitz—in the world of the death camps—where Israel was wrought.

"Father," said Levin.

Joseph turned his face away. "Father" meant nothing. He had probably turned himself away from a human sound. The back of his head was patchy. It looked like half a haircut, as if they had tried to clip his hair before he drove them away. Half a haircut. It reminded Levin of a doomed, shaved head. It disgusted him.

He had been at this point before. He had his pistol under his jacket. This time, he took it out. What would they do to him? Jail him for six months, if that? He wouldn't be the first to help a loved one out of his misery. Anna would have agreed to it. The back of Joseph's head begged for it, a bullet.

Levin put the gun away under his jacket. Not enough nerve. Maybe, in the last instance, not enough love. He left Joseph and walked back through the corridor, not glancing at the stranded shells in their wheelchairs. He felt very lucky. Deborah would be coming to him at the end of the week, which was something to look forward to.

In Jerusalem, that was all you could ask for.

ACKNOWLEDGMENTS

Joel gives thanks to Tel Aviv friend Helen Schary Motro who kindly read the novel for accuracy of local detail, to Lynda and Jill for early readings and support over the years, and to agent Philip Spitzer for finding the novel a home with Europa Editions. His wife Dorothy thanks Kent Carroll and his staff at Europa who walked her through the process of getting Joel's work into print.

About the Author

Joel Stone was born in Brooklyn. He graduated from Princeton University and was a Fulbright Scholar at the Sorbonne. His first novel, *A Town Called Jericho*, was published in 1992 and nominated for a Pulitzer Prize. He died in 2007 and is survived by his wife, the poet Dorothy Stone.

Carmine Abate
Between Two Seas
"Abate populates this magical novel with a cast of captivating, emotionally complex characters."—*Publishers Weekly*
224 pp • $14.95 • ISBN: 978-1-933372-40-2

Stefano Benni
Margherita Dolce Vita
"A modern fable...hilarious social commentary."—*People*
240 pp • $14.95 • ISBN: 978-1-933372-20-4

Timeskipper
"Thanks to Benni we have a renewed appreciation
of the imagination's ability to free us from our increasingly mundane surroundings."—*The New York Times*
400 pp • $16.95 • ISBN: 978-1-933372-44-0

Massimo Carlotto
The Goodbye Kiss
"A masterpiece of Italian noir."—*Globe and Mail*
160 pp • $14.95 • ISBN: 978-1-933372-05-1

Death's Dark Abyss
"A remarkable study of corruption and redemption
in a world where revenge is best served ice-cold."
—*Kirkus* (starred review)
160 pp • $14.95 • ISBN: 978-1-933372-18-1

The Fugitive
"The reigning king of Mediterranean noir."
—*The Boston Phoenix*
176 pp • $14.95 • ISBN: 978-1-933372-25-9

Steve Erickson
Zeroville
"A funny, disturbing, daring and demanding novel—Erickson's best."
—*The New York Times*
352 pp • $14.95 • ISBN: 978-1-933372-39-6

Elena Ferrante
The Days of Abandonment
"The raging, torrential voice of [this] author
is something rare."—*The New York Times*
192 pp • $14.95 • ISBN: 978-1-933372-00-6

Troubling Love
"Ferrante's polished language belies the rawness of her imagery, which
conveys perversity, violence, and bodily functions in ripe detail."
—*The New Yorker*
144 pp • $14.95 • ISBN: 978-1-933372-16-7

The Lost Daughter
"A resounding success…Delicate yet daring, precise
yet evanescent: it hurts like a cut, and cures like balm."
—*La Repubblica*
144 pp • $14.95 • ISBN: 978-1-933372-42-6

Jane Gardam
Old Filth
"Gardam's novel is an anthology of such bittersweet scenes,
rendered by a novelist at the very top of her form."
—*The New York Times*
304 pp • $14.95 • ISBN: 978-1-933372-13-6

The Queen of the Tambourine
"This is a truly superb and moving novel."
—*The Boston Globe*
272 pp • $14.95 • ISBN: 978-1-933372-36-5

The People on Privilege Hill
"Artful, perfectly judged shifts of mood fill *The People on Privilege Hill*
with an abiding sense of joy."—*The Guardian*
208 pp • $15.95 • ISBN: 978-1-933372-56-3

Alicia Giménez-Bartlett
Dog Day
"Delicado and Garzón prove to be one of the more engaging sleuth teams
to debut in a long time."—*The Washington Post*
320 pp • $14.95 • ISBN: 978-1-933372-14-3

Prime Time Suspect
"A gripping police procedural."—*The Washington Post*
320 pp • $14.95 • ISBN: 978-1-933372-31-0

Death Rites
304 pp • $16.95 • ISBN: 978-1-933372-54-9

Katharina Hacker
The Have-Nots
"Hacker's prose, aided by Atkins's pristine translation, soars [as] she
admirably explores modern urban life from the unsettled haves to the
desperate have-nots."—*Publishers Weekly*
352 pp • $14.95 • ISBN: 978-1-933372-41-9

Patrick Hamilton
Hangover Square
"Hamilton is a sort of urban Thomas Hardy: always a
pleasure to read, and as social historian he is unparalleled."
—Nick Hornby
336 pp • $14.95 • ISBN: 978-1-933372-06-8

James Hamilton-Paterson
Cooking with Fernet Branca
"Irresistible!"—*The Washington Post*
288 pp • $14.95 • ISBN: 978-1-933372-01-3

Amazing Disgrace
"It's loads of fun, light and dazzling as a peacock feather."
—*New York Magazine*
352 pp • $14.95 • ISBN: 978-1-933372-19-8

Alfred Hayes
The Girl on the Via Flaminia
"Immensely readable."—*The New York Times*
160 pp • $14.95 • ISBN: 978-1-933372-24-2

Jean-Claude Izzo
Total Chaos
"Izzo's Marseilles is ravishing. Every street, cafe
and house has its own character."—*Globe and Mail*
256 pp • $14.95 • ISBN: 978-1-933372-04-4

Chourmo
"A bitter, sad and tender salute to a place equally
impossible to love or to leave."—*Kirkus* (starred review)
256 pp • $14.95 • ISBN: 978-1-933372-17-4

Solea
"[Izzo is] a talented writer who draws from the deep,
dark well of noir."—*The Washington Post*
208 pp • $14.95 • ISBN: 978-1-933372-30-3

The Lost Sailors
"Izzo digs deep into what makes men weep."
—*Time Out New York*
272 pp • $14.95 • ISBN: 978-1-933372-35-8

A Sun for the Dying
"Beautiful, like a black sun, tragic and desperate."—*Le Point*
224 pp • $15.00 • ISBN: 978-1-933372-59-4

Gail Jones
Sorry
"In deft and vivid prose...Jones's gift for conjuring place
and mood rarely falters."—*Times Literary Supplement*
240 pp • $15.95 • ISBN: 978-1-933372-55-6

Matthew F. Jones
Boot Tracks
"I haven't read something that made me empathize with
a bad guy this intensely since I read *In Cold Blood*."
—*The Philadelphia Inquirer*
208 pp • $14.95 • ISBN: 978-1-933372-11-2

Ioanna Karystiani
The Jasmine Isle
"A modern Greek tragedy about love foredoomed, family
life as battlefield, [and] the wisdom and wantonness
of the human heart."—*Kirkus*
288 pp • $14.95 • ISBN: 978-1-933372-10-5

Gene Kerrigan
The Midnight Choir
"The lethal precision of his closing punches leave
quite a lasting mark."—*Entertainment Weekly*
368 pp • $14.95 • ISBN: 978-1-933372-26-6

Little Criminals
"A great story...relentless and brilliant."—Roddy Doyle
352 pp • $16.95 • ISBN: 978-1-933372-43-3

Peter Kocan
Fresh Fields
"A stark, harrowing, yet deeply courageous work
of immense power and magnitude."—*Quadrant*
304 pp • $14.95 • ISBN: 978-1-933372-29-7

The Treatment and The Cure
"A little masterpiece, not only in the history of prison
literature, but in that of literature itself."—*The Bulletin*
256 pp • $15.95 • ISBN: 978-1-933372-45-7

Helmut Krausser
Eros
"Helmut Krausser has succeeded in writing a great
German epochal novel."—*Focus*
352 pp • $16.95 • ISBN: 978-1-933372-58-7

Carlo Lucarelli
Carte Blanche
"Lucarelli proves that the dark and sinister
are better evoked when one opts for unadulterated
grit and grime."—*The San Diego Union-Tribune*
128 pp • $14.95 • ISBN: 978-1-933372-15-0

The Damned Season
"One of the more interesting figures
in crime fiction."—*The Philadelphia Inquirer*
128 pp • $14.95 • ISBN: 978-1-933372-27-3

Via delle Oche
"Lucarelli never loses his perspective on human nature
and its frailties."—*The Guardian*
160 pp • $14.95 • ISBN: 978-1-933372-53-2

Edna Mazya
Love Burns
"Combines the suspense of a murder mystery with
the absurdity of a Woody Allen movie."—*Kirkus*
224 pp • $14.95 • ISBN: 978-1-933372-08-2

Sélim Nassib
I Loved You for Your Voice
"Nassib spins a rhapsodic narrative out of the indissoluble
connection between two creative souls inextricably
bound by their art."—*Kirkus*
272 pp • $14.95 • ISBN: 978-1-933372-07-5

The Palestinian Lover
"A delicate, passionate novel in which history and
life are inextricably entwined."—*RAI Books*
192 pp • $14.95 • ISBN: 978-1-933372-23-5

Alessandro Piperno
The Worst Intentions
"A coruscating mixture of satire, family epic, Proustian
meditation, and erotomaniacal farce."—*The New Yorker*
320 pp • $14.95 • ISBN: 978-1-933372-33-4

Benjamin Tammuz
Minotaur
"A novel about the expectations and compromises that humans create for
themselves...Very much in the manner of William Faulkner and Lawrence
Durrell."—*The New York Times*
192 pp • $14.95 • ISBN: 978-1-933372-02-0

Chad Taylor
Departure Lounge
"There's so much pleasure and bafflement to be derived from
this thriller by novelist Chad Taylor."—*The Chicago Tribune*
176 pp • $14.95 • ISBN: 978-1-933372-09-9

Roma Tearne
Mosquito
"A lovely, vividly described novel."—*The Times* (London)
352 pp • $16.95 • ISBN: 978-1-933372-57-0

Christa Wolf
One Day a Year
"This remarkable book offers insight into the mind behind
the public figure."— *The New Yorker*
640 pp • $16.95 • ISBN: 978-1-933372-22-8

Edwin M. Yoder Jr.
Lions at Lamb House
"Yoder writes with such wonderful manners, learning,
and detachment."—William F. Buckley Jr.
256 pp • $14.95 • ISBN: 978-1-933372-34-1

www.europaeditions.com

Michele Zackheim
Broken Colors
"A profoundly original, beautifully written work, so emotionally accurate that it tears at the heart. I read it without stopping."
—Gerald Stern
320 pp • $14.95 • ISBN: 978-1-933372-37-2

Children's Illustrated Fiction

Altan
Here Comes Timpa
48 pp • $14.95 • ISBN: 978-1-933372-28-0

Timpa Goes to the Sea
48 pp • $14.95 • ISBN: 978-1-933372-32-7

Fairy Tale Timpa
48 pp • $14.95 • ISBN: 978-1-933372-38-9

Wolf Erlbruch
The Big Question
52 pp • $14.95 • ISBN: 978-1-933372-03-7

The Miracle of the Bears
32 pp • $14.95 • ISBN: 978-1-933372-21-1

(with **Gioconda Belli**)
The Butterfly Workshop
40 pp • $14.95 • ISBN: 978-1-933372-12-9